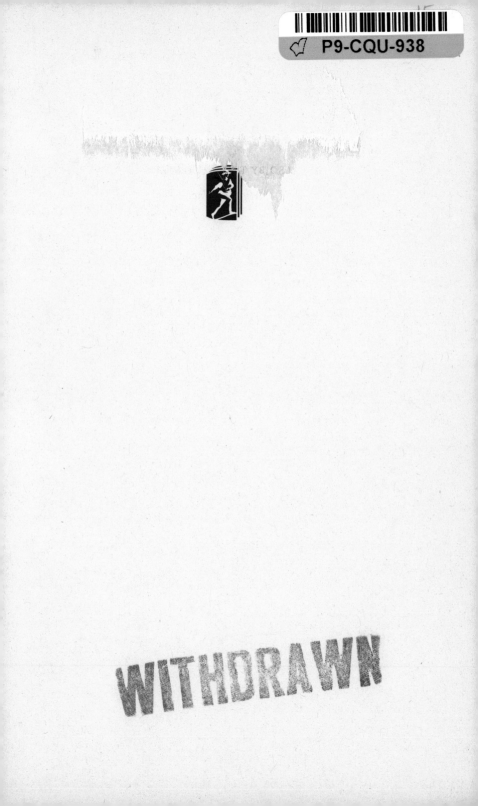

ALSO BY T. J. FORRESTER

Miracles, Inc.

Black Heart

on the

Appalachian Trail

T. J. FORRESTER

Simon & Schuster Paperbacks
New York   London   Toronto   Sydney   New Delhi

Simon & Schuster Paperbacks
A Division of Simon & Schuster, Inc.
1230 Avenue of the Americas
New York, NY 10020

First Simon & Schuster trade paperback edition October 2012

SIMON & SCHUSTER PAPERBACKS and colophon are registered trademarks of Simon & Schuster, Inc.

For information about special discounts for bulk purchases, please contact Simon & Schuster Special Sales at 1-866-506-1949 or business@simonandschuster.com.

The Simon & Schuster Speakers Bureau can bring authors to your live event. For more information or to book an event contact the Simon & Schuster Speakers Bureau at 1-866-248-3049 or visit our website at www.simonspeakers.com.

Designed by Jill Putorti

Manufactured in the United States of America

10 9 8 7 6 5 4 3 2 1

Library of Congress Cataloging-in-Publication Data

Forrester, T. J.
Black heart on the Appalachian trail / T. J. Forrester
    p. cm.
1. Hikers—Crimes against—Fiction. 2. Appalachian Trail—Fiction. I. Title.
PS3606.O74865B53 2012
813'6—dc22

                                                                        2011048689

ISBN 978-1-4391-7561-3
ISBN 978-1-4391-7563-7 (ebook)

This novel is for those who believe
they have the power to change their lives

Black Heart

on the

Appalachian Trail

1

HAWKINSVILLE, WYOMING—KING OF nowhere—
civilization's intrusion into mesquite, cacti, sand, and rattlesnakes. I grew up here, never thought I'd return, yet here I am. I
stretch out my legs, wriggle my prison-issue shoes to release the
crimp on my heels, peer out the bus window at a man on the sidewalk. Sunlight bounces off a wine bottle—MD 20/20—cheap,
nasty, buzz guaranteed. Between the man's feet, a dog licks at a
brown puddle. Vomit, I assume.

I make my way to the front and down the steps. The feed store
butts up to the terminal, and the air smells musty as a compost pile.
A settled-in smell, a going-nowhere odor, and it's the same as the
day I left.

The driver drags suitcases from the luggage compartment
and sets them at his feet. I give him my claim ticket—Taz Chavis #650–569—and tell him the duffel bag is mine. I'm traveling light. Eight-day trip. Three days coming, two days here, three
days going.

The driver hands me my bag, and I step around the man on

the sidewalk. The dog shows his teeth, two rows of yellow canines, and I lash out with my foot. Miss. A snarl, and the dog sidles out of range.

"Stupid mutt," I say.

I walk past the courthouse in the square, the barbershop on the corner, the Mercantile Bank next to Rexall Drugs. On a bench outside the Dollar Store, old men huddle like birds on a wire. A breeze, grittiness that abrades everything it touches, blows off the desert and down the streets.

Four blocks along I stop in front of Roy's Tavern. I spent my evenings watching my father through these windows. Dressed in a hat, suspendered jeans, and unlaced tennis shoes, he played nine-ball seven nights a week. He wasn't much of a drinker, sipped Pepsi from a frosted mug most of the time, traded it for the occasional beer but he never drank enough to get drunk. Probably a good thing. As many pills as he was taking, an addiction that began as a prescription for a nagging back, his heart would have quit working and he would have dropped dead on that wooden floor.

The saloon door, a refugee from an old-time establishment, had been jimmied so it swung inward; a concession to residents who complained about exiting drunks knocking sober citizens off their feet. That door . . . I hated that door and its physical imposition between me and my father. Some evenings I imagined it was my portal to manhood and in my dreams flung it open and exclaimed, "Pop, rack 'em up." But I never did. I knew better than to bother my father when he was at the pool table.

* * *

Pop was county dogcatcher, and he drove a pickup that had a cage on the bed. At the pound it was his responsibility to kill unclaimed animals. He called the gas chamber Canine Auschwitz, and his tone was without humor. His job led him to the dope—my opinion—but my mother put his problems to hand-me-down blood, said his father got hooked on opium in San Francisco and to watch out or I'd wind up like both of them. She ran off with a ranch owner who sold out and had money to burn. She sent me Christmas presents from towns in Arizona, Maine, South Dakota, Michigan, and Colorado. I appreciated her effort, but the presents were coloring books and toy trucks, like she didn't know I was growing up. Pop told me she died of ovarian cancer. Town rumor had her falling off a skyscraper or suffocating in a mine collapse in West Virginia. I settled for death by skyscraper. There was something romantic about plummeting through the air while the earth approached at an exponential rate.

"My father used to come here," I say, noting the space the pool table once occupied. I've gone through two pitchers and started on my third. Maria, a barfly who wandered over soon as I pulled up a stool, murmurs appreciatively, something she's done since I slid the first beer her way. Maria wears her hair away from her forehead. She has a broad face, brown as toast, wears a necklace made out of tiny turquoise stones. I look toward the window and think about my father. How did he feel about my nose always pressed to the pane? Mother said I had his hair, his eyes, his jaw.

She said I had a Chavis jaw, strong like a bull. Did my father see himself in me? Did he brag about his boy?

Maria stuffs the bottom of her blouse into her jeans and limps, cowgirl boots scraping the floor, toward the jukebox. She plunks four of my quarters into the slot, pushes a button, and a dusty old song fills the room. I guzzle beer and listen to her stumble over lyrics about skinning bucks and running trot-lines. When she hits the part about surviving, I nudge her chair closer to mine. She sits, and I rest my hand on her thigh.

"Drink up," I say.

She lifts her beer, takes a healthy swallow, puts the mug on the bar. "You're a little skinny. You sure you don't have AIDS or something?"

"Prison food, it'll starve a man to death."

"Three hots and a cot," she says.

I pour her a full one and listen to her tell about life back in Fort Redshire. I tell her I've never heard of that town and she says it's too small for the map. She says she grew up there.

"One time," she says, "I fell and broke my arm when I was riding my pony. Snap, just like that. One snap is all it took. . . . You may not believe it to look at me, but I have fragile bones."

"Life's a bitch."

"What are you talking about?" she says.

"I'm drunk."

"Me too."

She looks down at my hand.

"That won't do me any good," she says. "Feeling my leg like that."

I withdraw and return to my beer. Cunt. Or maybe I've lost my touch. I don't know which, and don't care. Maria raps her leg, a solid sound.

"Walnut," she says. "Motorcycle accident down in Tulsa. Would have killed me if I didn't have my helmet on."

I move my hand to the other leg. It's warmer and softer and I'm damned drunk to have rubbed a wooden leg. The door, the one I have despised for so long, swings inward and the man from the bus terminal falls through the sunlit opening onto the floor.

"I'm thinking of getting a room," I say.

"We could go down to the Mesquite Motel. You know that one? It's got vibrating beds and pink wallpaper. Nicest in town."

"Did you say you knew my father?"

"I didn't catch his name, sweetie."

"Wesley Chavis. Friends called him Wes for short."

"Wes?" she says.

"Wes Chavis. He used to come in here when I was a kid."

"Oh, sure. I knew Wes. Everybody knew Wes."

Her tone makes me think she's lying, but I don't care. If she wants to get naked it's okay with me. We get up, and I take one last look around.

"Did you know my father?" I say.

"You already asked me that, sweetie."

"I'm fucking plastered," I say.

"Me too, sweetie."

We step around the man, open the door, and shuffle into the afternoon sunlight. She drapes her arm around my waist, and we lean on each other—walk up to where the dog sits on the sidewalk and pants like he's at the end of a long run. I tell Maria to wait a minute and I go into the bar and buy three pickled eggs. I come back and drop the eggs in front of the dog and he eats them in three gulps. "Let's go," I say to her. We walk up the street, and I don't look back.

*   *   *

In prison, I envied the guys who could sleep fourteen hours a day. Tony Dobson was one of those guys. One morning, while we dressed for breakfast, he asked how I wound up in the joint. We were in prison blues, buttoning our shirts, backs to each other in the six-by-twelve cell. I told him I was doing a year for dealing.

"Sold bootleg jeans out of a van, had a coke business on the side. DA dropped the bootleg charges but sent me up on the coke. I was getting by, you know?"

"Bastards gave me nine years for raping my secretary."

That was our first real conversation. Most of the time he slept, while I stared at the walls, picked at food, and tried to stay on good terms with the guards. I read books about the Appalachian Trail and imagined I was out in the wild instead of surrounded by bars. If I thought hard enough, I could transport myself to the mountains and spend hours a day with an imaginary pack on my back and an open trail in front of me.

Toward the end of my stretch I received a letter. I knew without looking it wasn't from anyone I'd met on the East Coast. I'd lived in Atlanta for seven years, and I'd met a lot of people. Few who would write me a letter. On the street, friends were like Styrofoam cups. Some got crushed, others blew out of sight. Nothing was permanent. A guy went to prison and a week later he never existed.

Roxie Scarborough, the girl I was living with before I got sent up, didn't even send me a letter. Not that I expected differently. Roxie moved through life so fast she was not about to put things on hold for a lover behind bars.

That night, as I lay in my cell bunk, I spent my time thinking

about what was inside the envelope. Whenever I slid my hand
under the pillow and picked at the flap, I felt buoyant—a man
floating into a new day—someone with places to go and things to
see. When I couldn't take it anymore, I lit a match and read under
a flickering flame. My father was dead. There was a will. I had
papers to sign—formalities—could I please come to Hawkinsville when released? Tony heard me cussing and asked what's the
matter.

"Nothing," I said. "Burnt my fingers on this damn match."

I tucked the letter in the envelope and put my hands behind my
head. Hawkinsville. I hadn't thought about that town in years.

Maria and I come to a tavern and go inside. Same as the first:
country music, cheap beer on tap, a couple of regulars humped
over the bar. I've decided to see the lawyer today instead of tomorrow, so I'm sipping coffee, doing my best to sober up. Maria
drinks beer and nibbles pretzels. We're at a table next to the window and through the grime I see that dog nosing the sidewalk.

"That dog," I say.

"Christ."

"That dog, it followed us."

"I'm worn out," she says. "I can't walk any farther."

Maria rolls up a pant leg. "Doctors wanted to give me one of
those titanium thingies, but I wanted one made out of wood."

"Looks heavy," I say, and pour cream into my coffee. I sip, add
more cream. Overhead, suspended from a mayonnaise-colored
ceiling, a fan turns slow circles.

"Do you want some meth?" Maria asks. "I can get us some
meth, cheap too."

"That dog, he'd be looking at the gas chamber if my father was alive."

"They don't do that anymore."

"What?" I say.

"They use drugs and a needle to put them to sleep."

I buy a bag of potato chips and take it outside. I say to the dog, "You are one lucky dog," then pour chips on the sidewalk.

Pop's sobrieties began January 1st and usually lasted a week. Sometimes two. He flushed his pills down the toilet and did sit-ups and push-ups every morning. His eyes cleared and he stopped nodding off when he came home from shooting pool. When I was six, he lasted almost eight months. My mother danced to rock and roll records, and I jumped up and down like my legs had Superman springs. My father brought home soda and peanuts, and the three of us curled up on the sofa and watched TV. Whenever one of them got up, like to pee or get more ice, I felt warm on one side and cold on the other.

One Saturday—this was one of those times when Pop was off the dope—he drove me into the desert to see wild horses. He knew a spring where the herd watered twice a day. Once in the morning. Once in the evening. We went in the evening because Pop liked to sleep late when he wasn't chasing dogs. We stood on the downwind side, in a sandy patch behind waist-high mesquite. Pop whispered.

"Watch when they come in," he said. "The stallions, watch the stallions. Always keep your nose in the wind, boy. Always be on the lookout."

I nodded, but I wasn't much interested in horses. I wanted a puppy, something I could pet and feed and let lick my face if it wanted.

After what seemed like forever, the herd browsed up and over a rise while two stallions circled toward the spring. One stallion was black, the other was chestnut. They stomped sand and tossed their heads up and down.

"Watch," my father said. "See how they've got their noses to the wind. See that? They're looking for danger."

"Stupid horses."

"Shush, you'll scare them away."

"I want a puppy!"

My father's hand, a backhanded blur, connected with my cheek and I tumbled onto the sand. I got up but stood off to the side. Later, on the way home, he bought me a soda and I put my head on his shoulder. He tousled my hair and called me a good boy.

Looking back, I suppose he was explaining his troubles. But then, he might have been telling about horses.

"Can you believe this?" I say, and show Maria the check. We're outside the lawyer's office, and she sits on the curb with her leg extended like she dares someone to run over it. An ice cream truck turns the corner and comes up the opposite lane. The dog squats ten feet away, gaze on my face.

"That's a ton of money," Maria says. "With money like that we could buy a car and drive to California. We could open an orange juice stand and sell fresh-squeezed orange juice. All you can drink. We'd make a million, I bet."

"That dog's watching me."

"Scat!" she says.

A ratty tail beats the sidewalk.

"It's like he knows what I'm thinking."

"They're smarter than people."

"Dogs," I say.

"This leg, it gets so heavy sometimes I wish I had a grocery cart. I'd put it in there and hop around behind it. Everyone would say, 'Here comes Maria the bunny hopper.' You never know what people will say. I'm on disability, did I tell you? Nine hundred a month. I got a room up on Roundtree Avenue, but the landlady, she don't allow any male visitors."

A man in a suit comes out of the lawyer's office and gets into a pickup. He drives off, hood ornament flashing like a mirror turned toward the sun. Down the way, a Mexican comes out of a clapboard shack and sits on the sidewalk. It's unusually warm for February, and it feels like spring is coming early this year. Whatever snow fell at this elevation is long gone.

"The lawyer gave me a letter," I say. "From my father."

"Open it."

"I did already."

"Oh."

"It says," and I skim the letter. "It says. . . . This is what he wrote—it says if he could do it over again, he'd never touch a single pill—he says he hoped I turned out all right—he says to do something good with the money."

"You look to me like you turned out all right."

"I'm all right," I say. "I'm doing all right. Got money I didn't have an hour ago."

"We're stinking rich."

I stare at her leg, nudge it with my foot. No way in hell she's getting any of this money.

"You're the first one-legged woman I've seen," I say. "There was a one-armed Mexican back in Atlanta but I didn't know her very well."

"Give it a rest, sweetie."

I stuff the letter in my pocket. "My father would have killed that dog."

"He hated dogs?"

"I'm not sure," I say. "I really don't know."

"You're not an ax murderer or anything like that? You wouldn't rape me and chop me into little bits?"

"That's a stupid question."

"Never mind," she says. . . . "You can carve your initials into my leg if you want."

We walk down the sidewalk. My duffel bag is gone, and I can't re-member where I left it. Maria asks if she can lean on my shoulder, and I tell her okay long as she doesn't step on my feet. The dog walks a foot behind my heels, close enough for me to smell his road-kill odor.

"Einstein," I say.

"Pardon me?"

"That's his name."

"Einstein?" she says.

"That dog's one smart dog."

"I think he likes you."

"You think so?"

Her eyes are big and round and soft. "I think he'd follow you anywhere."

In eighth grade, I started huffing shoe polish. No big thing. I did it three times a day: on the way to school, during lunch break, and later behind the gym while the other kids played sports in the grassy field. When my grades dropped, the counselor called me and Pop for a meeting. Pop was still high from the pills I'd seen him swallow that morning, and his eyes were so droopy it was all he could do to force them open. The counselor, this creep who wore bow ties every Monday, suggested therapy. I stared at a bobble-head Elvis on his desk. Then pushed the head and watched it bobble. I giggled like crazy. Like I couldn't stop. I giggled until my stomach hurt, and my throat burned.

On the way home, my father drove the pickup harder than normal. On the bed, the cage slid toward the cab when he braked, slid toward the tailgate when he accelerated. He had his hat off, and the pink spot where his hair was thinning gleamed with sweat.

"The counselor said we needed to spend more time together. Said your mother leaving and all that screwed you up in the head."

"NA meets every Wednesday," I said. "Down at the Methodist church. We could sit together and cry big fat tears."

"Don't be a smart ass."

He braked at a stop sign and waved an old woman across. She had her head down, and she pushed a cart filled with grocery bags.

"Paper or plastic," I said.

"Huh?"

"I'm thinking of getting a job. Down at Green's Grocery, maybe bagging—"

"Nope," he said. "I already got you a job. Come Monday, you get out of school you walk your sorry ass down to the pound."

From that point on, Monday through Friday I fed and watered dogs, cleaned the cages with a hose I coiled in the corner when I was done. Every other Friday I herded dogs down a hallway and into the gas chamber. Some dogs went with tails between their legs, others growled and snapped. My father shut the door, turned knobs, and stood in front of the porthole. I stood to the side and watched him reflect the struggle behind the glass. It was like watching a slideshow where one picture fades into the next. The first few seconds he was the man who left the house after eating cereal for breakfast, a man in a hat and untied shoes headed for his everyday job. As time progressed—time that felt like hours but was only a few stretched-out minutes—his body stiffened like he was resisting a strong wind. The skin on his face stretched and his jaw melded into something cold, hard, and immovable. I looked at him for as long as I could, then looked away, understanding that no amount of narcotics could blur what he was watching. When it was over, I saw another man altogether. But this was someone I recognized. His voice was brittle, his eyes held defiant shame. His movement, when he lifted carcasses and dropped them into the wheelbarrow, was slow and shaky. Someone needed to put their arm around him and tell him it was okay, but we didn't have that kind of relationship.

One Friday, he walked up while I huffed paint out of a paper bag during my break. It was a hot, clear day and I was sitting on the picnic table behind the pound and dreaming about anywhere but there. Mostly I thought about jumping a freight car and going wherever it took me. I never dreamed about what I would do when I got to where I was going. My dreams were leaving dreams.

"I need you inside," he said.

"I hate this."

He sat across from me and took off his hat, ran a finger around the brim. "They're just dogs, better off dead than running the streets."

"You hate it Pop, I can tell. You hate the living hell out of this job."

He went inside, and I huffed until that weightless feeling rushed over me and my mind felt like a cloud in the jet stream—fast moving and light—vapor held together by the weakest of bonds. The door to the pound swung open and smacked into the wall, a crack that made me jump, and Pop appeared in the opening and crossed his arms. His hat was squished down on his head, a look that would have been comical if it hadn't reflected his frustration. I got up and spoke in a voice too boyish for the moment.

"I'm outta here."

"Put that shit away and get your ass back to work."

I stared him down—took in his gray pants, the blood-stained gloves, how his collar was turned up to keep the sun off his neck, the firmness he always had above his eyes when he ordered me around—tried to think of a reason to stay. My gaze met his, and his forehead softened, a fluidity that seemed to slide down his cheeks toward his chin, and I think that's when he realized this might be the last time we would see each other. When he spoke, his voice held a fuzziness I had not heard since I was a child.

"Do you have any money?" he said. "Do you have enough to get by?"

I nodded and he took off his gloves and we shook hands. He tried to say something and the words caught in his throat. I turned and walked away, spoke over my shoulder when I got to the street.

"See ya, Pop."

I headed to Piper's Truck Stop, where I caught a ride with a trucker headed east. Those were the last words I spoke to my father. There was nothing left to say.

*   *   *

"There's a whole lot we could do with the money," Maria says. "It wouldn't hurt to dream a little. We could go on a cruise to Alaska, see some whales, maybe feed some sea lions."

The motel room is exactly as she described. Vibrating mattress and pink wallpaper. Her leg is propped against the wall within easy reach of the bed. She's showered, and her wet hair fans across the pillow. She wears bra and panties, both green, a floral pattern of tiny roses embedded in cotton. Einstein, outside on the sidewalk, scratches the door. I look from her to the door, at her, at the door. We pass a whiskey bottle back and forth.

"Listen to that retard," I say.

"We could fly out to Seattle and get on a ship. That's where those Alaska cruises start, right there in Seattle."

"I'm thinking about going for a long hike, maybe walk the Appalachian Trail end to—"

"Or we could go to the Bahamas. I happen to know they have some great cruising down that way."

I look at her stump, then stare at the wooden leg, tilt my head so I see it from different angles. Disconnected, the leg looks lonely.

"Hey," I say.

"What?"

"If we had a shipwreck we could use your leg as a life preserver."

"That's my sweetie," she says. "Now you're thinking."

"I think I'm going to give Einstein a bath. Buy some flea powder and give him a good dusting." I take my shirt off and sling it over a chair.

"We need us some meth. Something to get us revved up. I can fuck all night long on meth."

"Shut up about the meth," I say.

"Quarter's only forty—"

"Shut up!" I raise my hand like I'm going to backhand her. It's a bluff. I never hit a woman who didn't hit me first.

"You smack me around and you'll wake up tomorrow without a dick."

Taz Chavis walking around without a dick strikes us as funny and we laugh. When we settle down I tell her dope put me in jail and damned if I was going back.

"No dope. Got it?"

The softness leaves her eyes and annoyance takes its place. I'm no idiot. She offered love hoping I'd get her high, and now she's mad for wasting her time. *Tough luck* is what I think.

We lie on the bed without talking, then I remember about giving Einstein a bath. I coax him and his road-kill odor inside, to the bathroom, where I set him in the tub, wet him down, and work motel shampoo into his fur. He's angles and knobs, skin stretched over backbone and shoulders.

"Hold still," I say.

He quivers but his legs are stiff like he wants to run but has made up his mind to endure. I ask him if he wants some Wild Turkey, we have half a bottle in the other room, tell him to stay clear of the meth-head with the wooden leg. I tell him today is my last fling and tomorrow I'm flying straight. I tell him I have the money to fulfill a dream, and I'm not going to fuck up and go back to prison. I tell him Pop never dreamed, that he was an addict who killed dogs. I tell him the lawyer said Pop was high when he hid in his closet and shot himself in the head. I tell him Pop's better off, wherever he is. The dog cocks his head and lifts his ears. His eyes are wary, and I wonder if he feels like he's looking in a mirror. I scrub until the water swirling the drain turns clear. He shakes and droplets fly. I call into the other room.

"I think I'm going to order a pizza, something with meat on it. I bet he likes hamburger."

I look around the door. Maria's eyes are shut, and a rhythmic hum comes from her nose. I wipe off my hands, walk to the TV and turn it on loud enough to drown her out. The dog, smelling like fresh-picked blackberries, sidles to my side of the bed, curls around three times, and settles on the carpet. I call the front desk and ask if anyone still delivers pizza in this town, write down the number, make the call, and order a large with extra hamburger. I can afford the extravagance.

It's morning and my head hurts. I don't remember much about last night. Maria's gone and so is her leg. She took fifty bucks out of my wallet. That leaves me with change and the check. I suppose, if she thought she could get away with it, she would have stolen *it* too.

Einstein and I leave the motel room. The sky is gray, slow to wake after a night's sleep, but in the east flame crawls across the horizon. I've forgotten about desert sunrises, how they begin so far away and seem so alive.

I ask Einstein if he's hungry and consider his wag an enthusiastic yes. I have a hungry dog and a $9,000 check in my wallet. I have a headache and a cottony tongue—

In my peripheral vision, a fist appears. A punch that catches me by surprise. It's a wide loop that misses my chin and spins my ambusher in a circle. I smell sour breath, cheap wine, unwashed clothes. I see a head matted with dirty hair and recognize the man at the terminal. Maria, wearing a twisted smile, stands behind him.

"Told you," she says. "I told you he was stealing your dog."

"That's my dog," the man says.

Maria's eyes are twitchy, and she chews her lip. She's high, tweaking on my fifty.

"It's my dog," I say.

"Liar." The man raises his fist.

I remove change from my pocket and hold the coins palm up. It's enough for a bottle of MD 20/20.

"Have one on me," I say.

"He'll pay more," Maria says. "He'll pay a thousand dollars for this dog. He loves this dog."

The man throws another punch, a lazy arc. I duck and then I have him by the throat. Coins fall to the ground and Maria kneels and paws at the dirt. My words are flat and hard. "Do you know how many dogs I've killed?"

The man's eyes are unfocused, but Maria glares up at me.

"Seventy-seven," I say. "Do you understand? We gassed them. You ever seen a gassed dog?"

I release my grip and point toward the ground at my feet. I tell them that's all the money they're getting.

"Don't fuck with me," I say.

Einstein and I walk across the parking lot to a street that curves around a gas station and heads east. At an intersection that leads down a street to the house I grew up in, I jam my hands in my pockets and lean against a weathered light pole. The lawyer said the house is up for sale and I'll reap the proceeds if a buyer comes forth, but not to look forward to it anytime soon. One part of me wants to revisit my youth and one part of me says that's where my father blew off his head and I have no desire to see blood-spattered walls.

I turn away and take a road that crosses the city limits, where I step over a sand-clogged gutter and arrive at the cemetery. I shield my eyes, trying to see the bone-white headstones. The sun is over the horizon, and the desert is on fire. It's burning up. The dog trots back into town, and I follow him for a block—watch him turn into an alley without a backward glance. I don't blame him, know I'm not worth taking a chance on.

Instead of going after him, I think about the last time I was in this town. Back then, my dreams were all about leaving. It didn't matter where I ended up or what happened when I got there, so long as it was anywhere but here. Now, I'm leaving with a dream that has substance and direction, a dream that began while I was behind bars. I promised myself then, and I'm promising myself now: I will walk the Appalachian Trail end to end. Or die trying.

It feels good to have a long-range goal, my first ever, and my feet feel lighter as they contact pavement. For the first time since I can remember I have a reason to get up in the morning.

2

ONE MINUTE SIMONE Decker, enjoying Day Two of her thru-hike, watches a hawk windsurf the updraft and the next she wants to push Devon off the cliff. He sits beside her, eats a cracker and brushes crumbs into the abyss. The urge intensifies, and she smothers it with thoughts of how much she enjoys spending time with him, and how tonight they will pitch the tent and snuggle into their sleeping bags and talk about whatever. She enjoys his voice in the darkness, likes how it surrounds and caresses her with its easy tone.

Marveling at the absurdity, she allows her thoughts to dissipate and the urge to reappear. Devon, in that quiet way of his, talks about buying a house with a spare room. He wants a studio that faces east so he can catch morning light while he works on his drawings. She nods agreeably, aware that sitting next to someone on a cliff is an act of implied trust. Has he ever thought about pushing *her* off? Simone lays her hand on his back, applies the tiniest pressure. She studies his eyes, looking for a flicker of recognition, and in the end decides he is oblivious.

They swing their legs over the void, stare at the view that begins a quarter mile below their feet and spreads toward the horizon. It is early March, and the Georgia forest is stark and barren. She is in her late twenties, they both are, and she has the build of an athlete, strong bones and strong muscles left over from her gymnastic days when she was a teenager in Oklahoma. Her eyes are hazel, and Devon often comments on the gold flecks in her pupils. She thinks her jaw is crooked and her nose is too big, and her hair is too flat, but her lover never mentions any of those things. He's an aspiring artist and sixth-grade teacher on spring break, and she's a laid-off scientist who worked for Luctow Labs in Tuscaloosa for five years. They have been together four of those years, met at a cocktail party after she attended a downtown art exhibit one Saturday evening.

Today she wears a Nike shirt and has on long pants because they conceal her thighs, which are more solid than fat, but she lives with worry Devon will lose sight of the difference. Her lover is skinny and can eat all he wants and not put on weight. She wears his ring. The diamond is bright and hard and promises two people wish to live together forever.

"Do you think I'm a bad person?" she says, rising and backing away. She picks up her pack, an internal Osprey she selected because she likes how it fits against her back.

"You are a fire-breathing monster."

"Devon."

"Ask a ridiculous question, get a ridiculous answer." Devon has brown eyes behind thick glasses and the magnification gives him a serious look. They are the same height, something she thinks he finds annoying because she often wears two-inch heels when they go out.

"I almost pushed you off the edge," she says.

"Now you're talking crazy."

"It's happened before."

"With me?" He sounds surprised.

"With others."

She closes her eyes and sees a murder gene twisted inside her DNA. The gene looks thin and flexible, deadly, like a garrote wielded in experienced hands. She was seven when the gene first showed itself, on the edge of the quarry where she stood behind Bobby Heavenside. Bobby had a crooked leg and walked with a limp, did not like it when other kids poked fun at him. She was big for her age, often rode a red bicycle her father bought for her seventh birthday. The boy stiffened against her thrust, was so off balance he could not stop moving forward. She jerked her hand away, like it was on fire, and peered down at his tumbling body, listened to the shrillness in the air. She felt no remorse, only a hot hand and a numbing stillness inside.

There had been one more, a girlfriend shoved off the top deck of a parking lot, an act Simone tried to delude herself into believing was an accident, but she gave up after a while because she knew the truth about herself. Deep inside she carried the intense desire to push people over the edge.

Strangely, the desire came and went on its own, submerging and resurfacing like a demented creature that only needed to breathe once in a great while. In high school, the desire surfaced when she was in a gaggle of kids atop the bleachers during a football game. The urge was strong, but she was so worried about getting caught she was able to shove her hands in her pockets and walk away. That was the first time her rational mind took control, and it gave her hope for the future.

At Ohio State, she studied genetic biology and familiarized

herself with the intricacies of DNA, polymers and nucleotides, chromosomes and replication. She read the works of Dr. Bristow, a scientist who theorized that one secret of the human race is that every person is born with a genetic flaw that leads to his fall. His theory comforted her. It meant the deaths were not really her fault, but at the same time she felt depressed. If her desire was gene based, that meant it would linger until the day she died.

During that four years, the desire surfaced from time to time, never strong enough to act upon, and she was, more often than not, amused with herself afterward. Eventually, she felt so confident she had gained control that she began driving to the Appalachian Trail during her summers, often testing herself when she came up on hikers taking pictures on overlooks. With each successful interaction she became even more confident and often sat with the hikers and held conversations that lasted for minutes at a time.

Then, during a day hike in the Whites, the urge reappeared with such ferocity it left her shaken. The boy had turned toward her as she neared, had stepped away from the edge in a hurry. He had looked frightened, as though he had seen something in her eyes.

That was the moment she decided to seek out ways to force change. She experimented with Buddhism and Catholicism, then finally resorted to self-help books. Her favorite was *How to Become a Completely New Person in Twenty-One Days*, and she read it three times in a two-week period. Afterward, she affirmed, she wrote negative notes to herself and set them on fire, she adopted positive attitudes that turned every half-empty glass half full. Nothing worked.

Now, as she contemplates her earlier interaction with Devon, she's annoyed with herself. This is the man she plans to marry. Soon as the urge appeared, she should have gotten up and walked away.

That afternoon, Simone and Devon crest another mountain and arrive at an overlook, and he glances at her with curious eyes. He asks if she wants to stop and enjoy the view.

"I don't want to sit next to you," she says.

"You're serious about this?"

Simone tells him yes and they walk down the mountain, he in the lead, she lagging behind. She crouches to take pressure off an old knee injury, wishes he would slow down so she could keep up. He looks back from time to time, but in the end seems to drop whatever is on his mind.

Devon plans to hike to her first resupply point—Hiawassee, Georgia—a town sixty-four trail miles north of Springer. When she first heard he was joining her for the start of her thru-hike, a conversation that took place back in the winter when she was dehydrating food for her mail drops, she was happy. Now she's not so sure. She's not worried about pushing him off—long as she stays clear of him on ledges bad things won't happen—but she thinks he might try to take over her hike and make it his. He is a male, after all, and genetically they are more comfortable when they are in control. She stretches out her stride until she runs instead of walks. Catches him at the next switchback. They hike to the base of the mountain and drop their packs in a clearing.

"A fire would be nice," Devon says. "Be dark before you know it."

Her lover prefers camp chores to gathering wood because he

worries about getting lost. Getting lost never happens to Simone. She has a keen sense of direction, much keener than Devon's.

Knowing he will not stop hinting until she brings him wood, she walks out of camp, along a ridge interspersed with pines, poplar, and white oaks. Fiddleheads, green and slender, curl out of the ground, but higher up, where branches are without leaves, colors are muted slashes of gray and brown. An owl's hoot drifts through the trees. Against the sky, in the upper reaches of a scarred poplar, wings unfold and a feathered shadow glides through the forest, gone before she can raise a hand and offer a hello.

She picks up a branch and drags it behind her. Picks up another branch and adds it to the first. Head down, she walks a wide loop that takes her into an oak grove south of the campsite. She hoists herself onto a low-hanging limb, climbs high enough to see down into the clearing. In a fork gently buoyant under her weight, she watches Devon glance in the direction she has disappeared. He restakes the guy line at the rear of the tent, then restakes the guy line at the front. He's fiddling, something he does when he is nervous. She wonders how long before he cracks, and an hour later gets her answer when he walks to the edge of the clearing and shouts her name.

"Simone!"

Simone wants him to go after her, rooting for his love to trump his fear of the forest, knows she wastes her time. Devon sees the trail as a conduit through the unknown. Venture from the footpath and he is doomed.

"Simone!"

She turns away, toward where the sun falls below the mountains. An orange band stripes the horizon and above the band the sky is the color of washed-out purple. Toward the north, where the sky is darker, the first star appears. She imagines the star hovers over the northern terminus, wonders how many steps it takes to get there from here. Devon believes she chose this journey because she wants to put off their marriage. He calls her thru-hike a 2,160-mile procrastination. But he's wrong.

"Simone!"

She's here because she's convinced herself that no one can thru-hike the Appalachian Trail and be the same person as when they started. She hopes change will arrive like an erupting volcano, melting her genes so completely that when they cool she'll become someone else entirely.

"Simone!"

Devon turns on his headlamp and the beam cuts a swath through the darkness, illuminates trees in its white glow. Guilt seeps through her, a nausea that washes into her stomach. She feels her way through the limbs, to the ground and the hard-packed trail.

"Hey," she says.

"Over here!" Devon says, headlamp bobbing. "I'm over here!"

"I'm here." She walks into the clearing and gives him a hug.

He backs away. "I've been calling for hours."

"I got turned around but I'm back now."

"I can't believe you did that!"

"I didn't get lost on purpose."

"You never get lost."

He complains that it's too late to bother making a fire, so she gets down on her knees and follows him inside the tent, where she unwraps a banana-flavored PowerBar and chews slowly, hoping to avoid conversation. The tent, with its low ceiling and narrow walls, feels cramped tonight. Devon takes off his boots, and she wrinkles her nose at the smell of dirty socks.

They are silent for a long time. She closes her eyes and tries to sleep, opens them when he pulls up her shirt and traces a circle around her belly button. She stiffens, but he seems unaware of her reluctance. His fingers drift under her panties toward the mound between her legs. She's dry but moistening and at that precise moment—yes, right there, just the tip of the finger—no, she should say no, say it loud like she was taught in high school; "No means no; girls, say it like you mean it"—No!—but there is only yes, and the finger thrumming and her mind focused on the swollen button until she is there and nowhere else, submerged in that hot river pulling her to the precipice—just the tip, there, yes, please, just the tip, please Devon—and her back arching and her legs contracting and her toes curling and her breath harsh and unabated—don't stop, don't stop, please don't stop—and the free fall over the edge, and the magnificence and the pleasure and the transcendent energy of being there, only there. . . .

. . . . Her voice, when it comes, is low and guttural.

"You bastard," she says.

"You love it." He guides her hand toward his crotch, but she won't have it, any of it, aware this is the first time she has refused to reciprocate.

"You're not playing fair," he says.

Simone spins her diamond palm down and makes a fist, winces as crystallized edges slice skin. The time on the trail was supposed to bring them closer together, but the opposite has happened.

*   *   *

That night Simone wakes to rhythmic noise she can't place. The noise is insistent, drawing her toward consciousness. She gives in and opens her eyes. At first she thinks the noise is Devon rubbing his leg, then recognizes the sound for what it is. The rhythm speeds, and her lips form a shy smile. She has never heard him masturbate.

"Devon," she says.

The noise stops.

"Devon?"

His voice has a fake grogginess. "Huh?"

"Never mind." She straps on her headlamp, opens her trail guide, and muses over tomorrow's hike. In the forest an animal skitters through the brush. The footsteps are so light she can hardly hear them—probably a squirrel or a night bird, maybe a raccoon—but she'd have to look outside to know for sure. The air doesn't smell as bad as it did when she went to sleep. Devon's socks must be drying out.

"The light's in my eyes," he says.

"Sorry." Simone flicks off the headlamp and darkness returns. The animal in the brush has stopped or moved out of hearing range. She rolls over on her stomach.

"Devon?" she asks. "Hey, are you awake?"

No answer.

"I feel a little sore, same spot as yesterday," she says. "I think I might have to take some ibuprofen."

A rustle, and Devon's hand finds her back. He applies gentle pressure, and every so often she lets out an appreciative moan.

"Is that it?" he says.

"A little higher."

"There?"

"Hey," she says, eventually tiring of his touch. "Did I tell you there was a road crossing tomorrow?"

Simone hasn't the courage to ask him to get off the trail, not even sure she wants him to leave. Devon turns his back to her, and she does the same to him.

"I'm thinking about rearranging my summer," he says. "I'm thinking I'll stay on the trail for a while longer. Maybe hike another couple months."

"I thought you wanted to go house hunting."

"The house can wait."

Simone listens for sounds in the forest, thinks of owls winging through the night. She wonders what it feels like to soar above the trees.

In the morning, they eat breakfast and hike north, soon arrive at Woody Gap, where Highway 60 intersects the trail and runs down the mountain in opposite directions. A station wagon pulls off the road and a white-haired man gets out and hobbles toward Devon. The man has a narrow forehead, hooded eyes, hands that shake when he waves hello. He hands Devon a business card, who, in turn, hands it to Simone. Mr. Quinton calls himself a trail angel, and he has a house five miles down the mountain.

"Thru-hiker?" Mr. Quinton says, directing his question at Devon.

"Georgia to Maine," Devon says. "One step at a time."

"You livin' my dream," Mr. Quinton says. "I tried to hike her when I was a young man but I got this trick ankle that would have none of it. I hang back now and try to help you fellows out. Do what I can here and there. Shower's hot, got a couple rooms, beds to sleep on."

Simone moves up to where she is shoulder to shoulder to Devon. *She* is the thru-hiker in this duo. Devon is the tagalong.

"One step at a time," she says, "that's the only way to thru-hike a trail."

The man glances at her, refocuses on Devon.

"So, how about it? You want a ride in?" Mr. Quinton says. "Five dollars each coming off the mountain but you and your gal friend ride free coming back. . . . If you stay with me, I mean."

Devon says, "Sounds reasonable."

"I don't say it on my card, but I cook pancakes for breakfast. Not all mornings, sometimes I sleep in. Breakfast is five dollars each if you want it."

"What about a ride to the nearest airport?" Simone says.

Now she has the man's attention. Devon's too.

"You thinkin' about gettin' off, honey?" Mr. Quinton says.

"Just asking."

"I don't blame you one bit," he says. "It's a hard go out there. Wear you to a nubbin' no time flat."

Devon flops his arm around her and squeezes. "She gets grouchy at night but she's been pretty good so far."

Mr. Quinton produces a paper from a rear pocket, runs his finger over jotted notations. "I can never remember these figures. Let's see, shuttle to Atlanta run you a hundred twenty dollars. Pretty lady like you I'll knock off the twenty." Yellow teeth show between parted lips. "No offense, just trying to be helpful."

"I might have to stop and pee," she says. "You know us womenfolk, we got us these small bladders, no bigger than a thimble, really."

"Don't I know it," Mr. Quinton says. "I had me a wife who couldn't drive no more than fifty miles without wantin' to run out to the bushes. When a woman has to pee she has to pee."

"I could pee right here," she says. "Right here before God and country and this here highway."

The man says, "Don't let me stop you."

"You'd like that," she says. "Bet you come up here and hide in the bushes just to see hikers pee."

"Now see here," the man says. "There ain't no call for—"

She steps onto the highway, dashes through a gap between a semi and a glimmering Porsche. Devon is close behind. He catches up and tugs her Osprey, spins her around.

"That was rude," he says.

"Who was rude, him or me?"

"You don't have to be such a bitch," he says. "He was trying to be helpful, trying to make a living."

Simone, with a downward slice of her hand and a severe point of her finger, motions him up the trail. She watches him stalk out of sight, then pulls down her shorts, squats behind a bush, and lets loose a stream that sends a beetle scurrying across the leaves. She hops behind the beetle, urine splashing the leaves, her boots, everywhere but on that blue back. She gives up the chase, thinking if she had been born with a penis, then life would be different all the way around.

That afternoon she catches up to Devon as he sits outside Blood Mountain Shelter and reads the register. Granite ledges surround the peak, and she suspects Devon, who never stays angry long, will ask her to sit with him and watch the sunset. She prefers to walk on, down the other side of the mountain, to a lower elevation free of temptation. He hands her the notebook and pen, disappears inside the stone building to roll out his sleeping bag. She flips to an entry made in mid-February and reads about September Sunset and Lizard Boy, a couple who started their thru-hikes earlier than most, and who hiked through a cold snap the day they crossed this mountain. Then comes Gregarious George, a man who hikes with a copy of Robert Frost poems and writes about starry skies and clouds white as cotton. She skims forward, stops on trail names like Monkey Toes, Greasy Spoon, Riot Boy, Sweet Dreams, Strider, Dances with Ravens, and Sloppy Seconds. She comes to Devon's entry. *Devon and Simone passing through on the 7th of March.*

Her lover appears in the doorway, extends a finger and pushes his glasses up his nose, tells her he'd rather keep hiking.

"It's like a dungeon in there," he says. "Like sleeping in a horror movie."

"I hate my name." She's delighted he has changed his mind.

He rolls up his bag and crams it in his pack. "I like Simone."

"Never mind," she says. "I'm sorry I brought it up."

"No, really, why obscure who you are?"

"Come on, Devon. We're not talking about plastic surgery."

His voice has a helpless tone. "Please, Simone, I don't want to argue."

"Never Lost," she says.

"Excuse me?"

"Never Lost, my new name. Simone is history."

She crosses out Devon's entry and writes: *Simone solo-hiking the trail and renaming herself Never Lost. Me here. Me gone. See ya when I see ya!*

Devon says it is time for them to go and she looks at him, asks herself if he notices anything different about her.

*   *   *

Day Four of her hike, she crosses a road and ascends in elevation. Hardwoods give way to waist-high mountain laurel bushes. The air is clean and cool. She watches her quadriceps expand and contract, notes with satisfaction her shorts are already feeling looser around the waist, not so much they are in danger of coming off, but enough so that she thinks she is losing weight.

She comes up behind a hiker headed north. He's an older man, a slow hiker who started the same day as she and Devon. Christopher Orringer walks with his head down, plodding steps, and he starts his day early and ends it late. She and Chris O, which is his trail name, have talked a few times, and he is a widower with no kids, had decided to thru-hike before his body gave out and he wound up sitting in a nursing home for the rest of his life. He steps aside with a grunt and allows her to pass, which she does with a quick hello, knowing he's too out of breath for conversation.

An hour later the trail tops the ridge, and she sees Devon sitting on a ledge. The mountains are blue and ripple into the distance. Down in a narrow valley smoke curls above the trees and bends in the wind. She imagines a house, or a factory down there, a place where humans live out normal lives.

Devon faces the expanse, shaking his head, as if locked in silent debate. She gazes at the flat spot between his shoulder blades. Estimates the distance, twelve feet across gray rock, and takes a step his way, heel to toe, like Indians walked when they stalked these mountains. He grips the ledge, and his fingers whiten at the knuckles.

"I want you to come sit by me," he says.

Simone closes the gap one step at a time.

"It's beautiful," he says. "I love the azure tint."

He's shaking, doubting her love.

"It's my breath, isn't it?" His laugh is feeble and ends abruptly. "I knew I should have carried some mints."

"I can't believe you're testing me."

"We can fix this, this, whatever it is," he says. "It'll go away . . . therapy, whatever you need, we'll get it."

Simone raises her arm and in her mind sees the sudden shove, followed by the sprawl of his body into open air. She hears his scream, long and shrill, stops mid-stride, and backs up a step. The ring comes off in a single twist. She releases it into the air and watches it drop and bounce at her feet. His face pales, and his eyes open wide.

"You can catch a ride into town back on that highway," she says. "Plenty of cars coming by."

Simone jogs down the trail, bends her knees more than usual to reduce impact. She will not allow herself to feel sorrow for the breakup, hopes leaving Devon is the catalyst for the change she seeks, imagines DNA bubbles inside her cells, molecules heating and realigning, cooling into something benign. The scientist in her says this cannot happen, that she will remain who she is until she dies, but she ignores the thought, wanting, for at least one time in her life, to believe anything is possible.

3

MY ROOM'S OKAY for a hundred and fifty a week. I've lived in worse places in downtown Atlanta. An air conditioner blows cold wind across the bed, and on the wall I've hung a picture of a hiker on the Appalachian Trail. The hiker stands on a rock at the edge of a cliff and has a cocky smile. He's in Virginia, on McAfee Knob, and the mountains below are green as a fairway. A cloud floats in the sky, far off, a whiteness above the horizon. Next to him, above an empty bookcase, is a picture of a Maine chef with fingers wrapped around a lobster. The chef has contented eyes, like, if he cooks for the rest of his life, it's fine by him.

The pictures, motivational when I tacked them to the wall, now serve as a source of irritation. If I hadn't called Roxie Scarborough after leaving Hawkinsville, if she hadn't invited me for a drink so we could talk about old times, if I hadn't said yes, I'd already be on the trail. But here it is, closing in on April. It's almost a month past the start of thru-hiking season, and I'm still in town. I don't beat myself up about it. A guy should have the right to enjoy himself after spending a year in the pen, shouldn't he?

I stare at the pictures until the light through the window turns gray, go outside and drive the streets in a beat-up Buick I purchased with part of my inheritance. Tonight, the air is hot, a simmer that dries from inside out, and the asphalt, slick from a spring shower, glistens like a black mirror. I breathe exhaust fumes and watch the shadows. Heroin, crack, meth, coke, weed, acid, it's all there.

Both sides of the street, buildings jut into the sky, and signs high on concrete walls jerk on and off. Under branched street lights, women in jacked-up skirts strut the sidewalk. If a john barters with a whore in bad shape, blow jobs start at ten dollars. Barter with a whore in worse than bad shape, and five will do. I drive past a Salvation Army, past a tavern with an open door, past a massage parlor with iron bars on the windows.

A girl in a silver miniskirt waves me over. She has long legs, and she's stoop-shouldered, tall, a young woman embarrassed of her height. I pull to the curb and roll the passenger window all the way down. She leans inside, dreadlocks framing a narrow face, and a boob slips from its fold. She smells of sweat and smoke, and I wonder when she last took a bath.

"Taz, honey, you know Roxie would kill me for messing with you," Laketa says, and stuffs her boob behind her halter top. "She's down on Thirtieth Avenue. You know the house where TT Charlie hangs? He's got some good dope."

I remember something I saw under the passenger seat when I was vacuuming the floorboards, dig out a plastic raincoat, and stick it through the window.

"Look, Laketa, you stay dry, you hear. You sleep someplace warm tonight."

She shrugs into the raincoat, a grateful look on her face.

"Roxie ever turns you loose you come see me. I'll take care a you like you never seen."

I merge the Buick with the flow of traffic, tuck behind a minivan. Rain pelts the windshield, and taillights reflect off the street in long liquid lines. The humidity makes me wish for air conditioning, but that's too much to ask with this crap car. It has one amenity, a radio that gets elevator music—only elevator music. I dribble my fingers on the dash and nod my head to a sleepy piano solo. Call it destiny, fate, whatever, but I knew I was headed for the gutter the summer I left my father at the dog pound, hitched east, and got a job at a zinc extraction facility in southern Georgia. Third shift was quiet, the nights lit with stars, and I spent my time hiding from this greasy operator who constantly chased me down. He was bucking for a promotion. Moving up in the world, he said.

On the Thursday before my first payday, an hour into the shift, I was easing across the concrete pad when I stepped into a drainage ditch. Hydrochloric acid soaked through my pant leg and filled my boot. I giggled at the absurdity, one foot in the gutter, one foot out. I had a choice and knew it. I could pull the foot out, or step in with the other one. I sensed this was important, that the choice I made forecast my future. The operator whined for me to stop acting like an idiot and get out of there pronto. I looked at him, big-ass grin on my face, and stepped in with the other foot. He yanked me to the pad and hosed me off. I wasn't in long enough to bubble skin, but he said the acid would have eaten me to the bone.

That's what the gutter does to a guy, eats him to the bone.

*   *   *

Roxie is the kind who gets inside a guy's head, the kind who hits hard. We met in a bar on the south side a year after I moved to Atlanta. We danced to Meatloaf, and she asked if I wanted to party. She was too skinny for my tastes, but when I slipped her sleeve up her arm and saw the track marks, I knew she wouldn't mind me huffing paint now and then. We drove to an overpass that petered out on the other side, like the state ran out of money or a rich politician changed his mind, and right there, in drizzling rain, we screwed on the hood of her mother's Honda Civic. After that, we were inseparable, and I quickly traded my high for hers. Seemed like the natural thing to do at the time.

She's white trash, I suppose, although I think there's more to her. Sometimes, when I least expect it, she works an obscure word into the conversation. Like *titular*. She used that one time when she was off on a rant about the president. She's told me so many stories about herself I don't know which to believe. One day her father's a Methodist preacher who stuck his finger where it didn't belong, and the next he's CEO of Minute Maid. Supposedly there's a sister in Miami, or Houston, or New York, maybe Memphis. Like I said, the story changes day to day. Roxie's a habitual liar, but I don't care. What we had, what's between us now, is real as it gets.

I park in a rutted drive, weeds knee-high in the yard, get out, and walk to the back of the house. A woman steps through the door and merges with the darkness. A stumble, a curse, and she's gone. Inside, I pick my way down the cluttered hall, while breathing in a urine stench so strong it waters my eyes. In one of the bedrooms, a black man on a mattress, muscular legs expanding and contracting, humps a white girl, or maybe a white boy. I can't tell from this angle. I move on, down the hallway, to the kitchen. Crusted dishes clutter the sink, the counters, the refrigerator. A Mexican lies motionless on the floor.

A moan in the living room, and when I turn the corner, Roxie's naked on her knees in front of a guy on the couch. The guy's name is TT Charlie, and he's zipping his pants. I study her face, so familiar—the mole under her ear, the sliver of a scar on her cheek, the fine black hairs above her lip. Her eyes are my favorite part. They are a green paradox—innocently hard—eyes with staying power.

TT Charlie nods in my direction, then says, "I got me some bad-assed Peruvian Pink Lady if you're interested. Ain't cheap. Sixty a quarter."

"I'm all right." I watch a hooker I don't know stumble into the room and sit in the recliner in the corner. She hikes her dress to her waist and spreads her legs wide as a wishbone. Her panties are yellowed in the crotch, and curly black hair, tight as a wire brush, grows on the inside of her thighs.

"White boy," she says to me. "Blow job'll cost you ten, poontang's twenty-five."

TT Charlie pushes Roxie away and hands her a quarter-gram. She pulls on hip-huggers and a red blouse, comes over and gives me a hug.

"I need to talk to you," I say. "About something important."

The woman in the recliner says, "You watch out, girl, that white boy's vice through and through. You watch out or he be running you up town. I seen his kind coming and going. He put you in jail and now where you gonna be?"

"Shut up, Fayesha," TT Charlie says. "Taz ain't no vice. That's his old lady."

"All I'm saying," Fayesha spits, "is she should watch her ass. I seen his kind. He don't want no poontang, he don't want no dope, there's something wrong. That's all I'm saying."

"That Mexican out on the kitchen floor might be dead," I say.

"We got us a real genius here," TT Charlie says. "A real community-college whiz. That watermelon picker's been dead since morning. We ain't got around to it yet."

"It'll cost you," Roxie says. "Me and Taz'll dump him for an eight-ball."

"Ditch his petrified ass away from here," TT Charlie says, "and you got a deal."

I drag the Mexican out of the backseat and roll him into an alley that backs up to a shopping mall. Roxie fires her lighter, and the Mexican's eyes shine like white buttons. I cover his face with a soggy newspaper and look away. The southern terminus of the Appalachian Trail, less than a hundred miles to the north, feels like it is so far off it might as well be in another galaxy. I want to blame Roxie, the hold she has on me, but know I am at fault too. This life—filled with dead addicts, prostitute girlfriends, the intense desire for a fix—is a weakness I've never overcome.

"He might have some dope," I say. "Feel down around his balls, unzip and feel down there, and see if he has some dope."

"I'm not feeling up no dead man."

"Feel down there and see if he has some dope. He must've died from something. Poor bastard probably overdosed."

"TT Charlie checked him over pretty good. He didn't have no dope and he didn't have no money, no ID, nothing but one of those Spanish phone calling cards. Fayesha says his name was

Julio and he was a wetback that worked down at Pizzaria. She said he hadn't eaten in two weeks, probably starved himself to death or his heart stopped or something."

To the south, lightning, like a radioactive vein, branches across black sky.

"I got something in the trunk, a surprise," I say.

"If I'd known he hadn't eaten in two weeks I would have brought him a sandwich, or something. Maybe an egg roll. Huh, Julio? You think you might have liked an egg roll?"

"I have this plan, to get out of here, go somewhere we can't get any dope. It's impossible to get dope where I want to go."

Roxie unzips Julio's pants, feels under his testicles, and comes up empty. "The things I do for you."

I open the trunk.

"See, I went to an outfitter and bought a backpack and a sleeping bag and a stove and hiking clothes, and look here, a book about a crippled guy who hiked the Appalachian Trail. I must have read this fifty times when I was in prison. If a guy with a bad leg could do it, it'd be a piece of cake for you and me."

She holds the book to the trunk light. "You nuts? I told you I ain't walking no Appalachian Trail."

"I'm talking about walking out of here up to Maine and I'll get a job as a cook and maybe we'll wind up near the beach and I'll fish for lobsters. You can't get dope on the trail, that's what I'm saying. There's no dealer setting up in the mountains. You can't get dope out there. It's a dope-free zone."

"You ain't no cook."

"I can learn," I say. "It can't be that hard."

"You can't even cook eggs."

I can cook eggs, but I don't want to argue the point.

Roxie gets in the passenger seat, and I wait outside while she shoots up. Then I head to 7-Eleven and buy donuts, broiled sausages, and a jumbo package of potato chips. Roxie's quiet when she's high—like she has too many thoughts to sort through— but I don't mind. It wouldn't kill her to offer me some of that eight-ball, she'd still have plenty left for the early-morning hours. My hands clench the steering wheel. Whenever a craving creeps through my body, I think about the trail. I don't know if I'll like walking through the mountains or if I'll like sleeping on the ground, but I can walk into any town in the lower forty-eight and buy coke within the hour. Can't do that in the mountains, and that's what I'm saying. There is no gutter on the Appalachian Trail.

The Buick's headlights sweep across earth brown as coffee stains, and the trailer, caught in the gleam, shines like an aluminum coffin. I park in the driveway, and Roxie and I get out and walk to the door. A barbecue smell lingers in the air, and I'm reminded of the food we purchased at 7-Eleven. That's another thing that's different since I quit shooting coke. Once I got clean in prison I started thinking about food all the time. Especially chocolate. There's nothing like an oversized chunk of chocolate melting in my mouth. I swear it makes me hard. I'm cut out for food. That's why cooking up in Maine's a good idea. I can make it as a cook. I bet I have recipes I never thought of.

"You coming in or what?" Roxie says.

The door thumps the siding, and windows vibrate. I lug the backpack inside, set it on the floor. The trailer is single-wide and has a kitchen and combination living-dining room. There are a few pictures on the walls, an ashtray on a chipped end table, a red couch that faded to orange a long time ago. I glance at the refrigerator and can't help but smile at a picture of a Greek ruin. Roxie dreams about traveling abroad, and she clips *Atlanta Journal-Constitution* articles about exotic cities. She has plans to work for a travel agency that sends employees around the world, says she knows so much about these cities that she will make an excellent guide. I'm glad to see she's still dreaming and turn her way.

"Help me with this, will you?" Roxie melts coke on a spoon, cinches a shoestring around her bicep, and grips the string in her teeth. She's been pumping these veins for ten years, and purple splotches mottle the inside of her elbow like chicken pox. I press the needle through her skin and find a vein on the first try. Her teeth unclench, the string releases its grip, and her eyes roll back.

"This is some good dope," she says. "Hits like a train."

I open the backpack and hold up a miniature radio I bought especially for Roxie because she likes her music.

"See," I say. "This thing runs on AA batteries and we can share it at night. You can listen to your country and I can listen to jazz."

Roxie rolls up my sleeve. She's offering to get me high, and I might as well admit it, the coke in that Baggie is killing me. I want it so bad my heart's clenched hard as a baseball. The doorknob down the hall turns clockwise, then counterclockwise, then clockwise. Click . . . Click . . . Click . . . Click . . . A circular metronome.

"Damn!" Roxie says. "When she went out, she must have locked Odell in the bedroom."

"What the fuck?"

I have no idea who is down there, so I ease my way toward the kitchen and rummage through a drawer for a knife. Roxie tells me to relax, that a girl she met over on Fifth Street is staying for a few days. The boy is only four, and he's probably hungry.

"His grandmother is picking him up in the morning," Roxie says. "Brittany only has him every other weekend."

"Where the hell is Brittany?"

Roxie shrugs, and I know my answer without prying. Roxie's roommate is a hooker out making money for her high. I jog down the hall, open the door to the rear bedroom. There's bottled water on a dresser, and in the corner a bucket for a toilet. The room smells like a gas station bathroom. Odell darts past my leg, and I follow him to the table. Wrappers fly. He stuffs a wrinkled sausage in his mouth. The kid's got shaggy brown hair, a rock star look, and squinty blue eyes. He wears shorts, no shirt, and ribs show through skin like rows of bent branches. He chews through three sausages, starts in on the potato chips. The boy eats like it's going out of style. If I had a restaurant, I'd want it full of eaters like him.

"Eat up," I say.

"We got some box wine and a twelve pack of Old Milwaukee," Roxie says, and trickles me a glass of wine. I drink it and another. Odell falls asleep on the couch, and I cover him with a blanket, ask Roxie if I should carry him to the bedroom. She says the boy can sleep through anything and won't wake until morning, so I spread backpacking gear on the floor—tell her about the sleeping bag and how it has baffles to keep the down evenly distributed.

"It's a Mountain Hardwear 15 degree," I say. "Top of the line. . . . Too long for you but they sell a small that would fit you pretty good."

Roxie hands me a beer, but I put it on the table and tug her pants to her ankles. She pushes me away, shoots up again. Then she takes off her hip-huggers and walks around in blouse and panties. She throws the backpack over her shoulder and I'm pleased. She's into the idea, the first time I've seen her seriously consider my plan.

"*Moowhaaah*," she says, and bends at the waist. Head down, she stomps around the room. "*Mooooooowhaaaaaah*." She extends her index fingers and puts one on each side of her head. Her foot scrapes the carpet. "I'm a stoned-assed bull and you're the matador. Show me some ass, Mr. Matador."

I take off my shirt, my pants, my underwear, and she rams her head into my butt cheeks. Her fingers dimple my skin like pink worms. I laugh so hard my sides ache, lean over the table and roll the needle in a circle. One bump wouldn't hurt, might temper the zipper of a headache I'm sure to have tomorrow. I walk down the hall to the bathroom, relieve myself, then eyeball the mirror. I stick my fingers in the corners of my lips and pull the skin tight. Then I grab a brush on the counter and comb my curls across my forehead. Then I tease them straight up in the air. I should have been a frontiersman. I would have walked through the mountains and eaten meat on a stick every chance I got. I love meat on a stick. Chicken, beef, pork, name it, and I've eaten it on a stick. My stomach's stuck on spin cycle, and I puke bile into the rusty toilet bowl. If I want to get high, I better do it now. That coke's going fast.

Roxie cusses in the living room and I hurry in there and shoot her up. "These veins," she says. "These veins are like spaghetti. I got spaghetti veins. I'm a fucking bull with spaghetti veins."

I pick up the box wine and hold the spigot to my lips. Drain the box, toss it on the floor. Drain the last beer and toss it next to the box. The sun's coming up, and through the window the trailers look dirty in the brown light. A car drifts down the road. Some sucker headed to work, no doubt. In the yard across the way, a woman with curlers in her hair clips weeds around her mail box. Weeds! Who thinks about weeds first thing in the morning?

"Taz," Roxie says. "Taz, come here."

She tells me she spilled the coke, drops to her knees, rakes her fingers through the carpet. I think of the boy and can't remember if we fed him or what. He's asleep on the couch, and I don't know how he got there.

"Give it up," I say. "That dope's history—"

"You're such an asshole."

"I'll take you to get some more. Just relax and we'll go in a minute. Take a shower, why don't you? You smell like hell." My hands shake, and I stare at that needle.

"Get off my ass, don't nobody care how I smell. TT Charlie don't care and he's the only one that matters. He's got the dope, you ain't got shit. You got less than shit."

Instead of arguing, I let her believe what she wants. If Roxie knew about Pop committing suicide and leaving me an inheritance, she'd bleed me dry inside of a week. She opens the door, throws the backpack outside, and it rolls across the lawn and rests against a rimless tire.

"Cook, my ass," she says. "You ain't leaving me and I ain't walking no Appalachian Trail. You put your clothes on and take me to the corner. I'll get us some money and we'll get us some coke and come back here and do it up. You and me, we'll do it up like old times."

At the window I study my backpack. The dirt is wet with dew and the sun is coming up. It will be a hot one today, and I look around for a fan. There's the needle, the empty Baggie, a dozen empty beer cans, the noise from the shower, and Odell on the couch. Breakfast coming up, I say in a voice too loud. I heat a skillet on the stove and get four eggs out of the fridge. I break the eggs over the skillet and watch the whites bubble and brown on the edges.

I set full plates on the table, walk out the door, and rummage through the backpack for my hiker clothes. I put them on and stand around in the dirt. It feels odd wearing shorts and trekking shoes, a T-shirt made out of something other than cotton. I strap on the pack and walk around the car, imagine I'm on the trail, try to smell the woods after a rain. The only odor I pick up comes from an overflowing trashcan in front of the adjacent trailer. Roxie appears at the door. Odell stands beside her and brings his knuckles to his eyes.

"You make sure his grandmother knows his mother locked him in that bedroom," I say. "You make sure he's fed."

She nods.

"Come inside," she says.

Roxie is the most beautiful woman I have ever seen. Cheekbones, the green eyes, the cocked-hip attitude, I must be crazy for thinking about leaving her.

I get in the driver's side, drop the backpack into the passenger seat, crank the sleepy piano music up as loud as it will go. The door speakers rattle and the pounding itches my eardrums. I am older, wiser than when I stepped in the acid in that extraction facility. I slam my hand on the dashboard, a smack that jolts my arm clear to the shoulder.

Fuck that gutter.

4

LEONA BROUGHAM ENTERS the attic and walks up to a sofa she and her husband had retired years ago, extends a finger and smudges SOS in the dust that coats the broken arm. She had been so certain their lives would unfurl in a way that would keep them together until the end. Now, with Emanuel joining Swingers In Their Golden Years to spice up their sex life, she thinks she might end up alone. Sex life? That part of their marriage ended years ago, along about the time he began snoring so loudly she was forced to sleep in another room.

She plops a box on the sofa and dust mushrooms into the air. Inside, under the knickknack clutter, wrapped in a towel for safekeeping, lies a cassette tape Emanuel recorded during his Vietnam tour. Leona has listened to the tape three times in her life: once when it arrived; once when she got the seven-year-itch and almost ran away with Trevor, chief editor where she worked at Howell Publishing all those years; and once when she was thirty-seven and her husband had an affair. She never discovered the woman's name, but the lipstick on his collar, the perfume on his body, his propensity to shower before pecking her cheek and saying hello, added up to nothing good.

She drops the tape in her pocket and makes her way down the steps, walking carefully so she doesn't aggravate her joints. In the living room, Emanuel relaxes in a recliner in front of the television. His head turns toward the bay window, where the trim frames New Hampshire mountains that rise out of the ground like great humpback whales. A hot spring has burned off the snow, and craggy boulders etch the sky. A million thaws have eroded the peaks—splitting fissures until rocks gave way and rolled into valleys—yet the mountains are still here, still strong—a longevity that stirs her soul.

Leona studies the profile, knowing it well, harking back to when she tromped the Appalachian Trail on summer weekends, carrying hoes and pruning shears, digging water bars, and cutting back the growth to offer clear passage to hikers. Now she feels old as the trail and leaves the job to the younger crowd. The Appalachian Mountain Club honored her with a dinner and plaque when she retired. She is not given to bragging, and the plaque resides in the top dresser drawer instead of hanging on the wall.

She pauses next to the fireplace and watches her husband. He is a proud man, especially of his height, and it galls him that he now tops out at five eleven instead of six foot. The shrinkage should have taken him down a notch in more ways than one, but what he lacks in stature he makes up for in hair. Not only does he have all of it, a dense wave that curls around his ears and sweeps toward his collar, it is the same color as the day they met. Yellow as a fall maple leaf, no gray to be found. He looks her way and shifts in his seat, tells her the Wasatch couple will be here any minute.

"For an interview," he says. "You remember, don't you darling?"

In less than an hour they plan to size up potential sex partners. Leona wonders how one should act in these situations. Should she flop out a breast and allow Mr. Wasatch a squeeze? Should she roll down her nylons and expose the pink between her legs? She glares in Emanuel's direction. Men and women their age should have better things to do.

Leona prefers taking her children's calls in the kitchen. This room, floor tile reflecting the fluorescent lights, was the center of her world when Heather and Parker were young, their orbits bringing them to the counter for help with homework, to the fridge for snacks, to their mother's arms for childhood bruises, real and imagined. Talking to her children on the phone brings those memories to life. If she closes her eyes, she can still smell cookie dough in the oven, still see birthday cards tucked under Mickey Mouse magnets, still hear the young voices chatter about anything from ants to the Man in the Moon.

At the breakfast nook, she adjusts the phone so it won't dig into her earring, says hello to her son. He starts right in on the elephants he's seen playing soccer in Thailand. Thailand? She never can keep up with her youngest. Parker, a sweet boy who inherited his father's hair, caught the wanderlust soon as he could crawl, and by the time he was three she'd had to leash him when she walked the grocery aisles. She blames his divorce on his restless spirit. Sometimes she wishes he was more like Heather, her oldest, who has lived in a small town outside Boston for the last twenty-five years. Least he'd come around more often.

"So, how are you?" he says.

She glances toward the living room where the Wasatches sit on the sofa. Mrs. Wasatch wears a slinky dress, mail-ordered from Macy's, and her high heels reveal tiny feet. Tiny feet irritate Leona, whose own are so wide she has trouble finding the right fit. Mr. Wasatch, three times the size of his wife, wears a Hawaiian shirt that does little to hide his belly. His wife worked as a bookkeeper for their hot tub company, and they both believe sitting in steamy water is good for the constitution.

"We're entertaining. The Wasatches are in the living room." Leona craves her son's company, and the strangers in her house amplify her feelings. She doesn't want to start crying, so she goes to the sink and runs water into the coffeepot. The mechanics of doing something soothes her. Parker is silent, and she knows he is trying to place the name. That's how it is between them. They talk on the phone and trade news. Try to fit it into the larger picture.

"Your father wants to start swinging," she says. "We're interviewing couples."

Emanuel calls her name, and she puts down the coffee filter. For the occasion her husband wears a long-sleeved corduroy shirt, a crosshatch of brown and green she gave him for Christmas several years back. He calls again, says Mrs. Wasatch requests bottled water. Bottled water? Brougham water comes out of the tap, no fancy shenanigans in this household. Parker chortles in her ear. She wishes she was there to see his head slant back and his belly jump in and out. Her son is a whole-body laugher, able to give all of himself to the humor of the moment.

"It's not *that* funny." Leona, who chose a pink blouse for the interview, forgot about a problem button that comes undone if she moves around too much. She buttons up and holds her stomach in. She is forgetting something. Oh, the tape. She forgot to listen to it, cannot remember where it wound up.

"Heather told me you two had gone wild," Parker says, "but I thought she was yanking my chain."

"It's your father. He's having another crisis."

Her son cackles, then settles down. "I expect next you'll order the Playboy Channel."

"Parker, you watch that mouth."

The phone hisses and pops, and she taps it in her palm. She knows it's unusual for a woman her age to share her sexuality with her children, but she began telling them everything about her life soon after they moved away. This desperate attempt to keep them close to her breast only works with Heather, who reciprocates by revealing things so intimate they make Leona blush. Parker holds back, has a reticence she blames on a gene passed from his father.

"I have to go," Parker says.

"You be careful around those elephants, don't get stepped on."

"Okay, Mom. I love you."

She says the words back, half a mind to ring Heather. Emanuel calls again, and she heads his way.

"Sorry," she says to the couple. "We're out of bottled water. I'm making coffee if you'd like some."

The Wasatches say caffeine elevates their blood pressures, and they swore off years ago. Mrs. Wasatch sports a face-lift, and she brags about her surgeon, believing he is top-notch. "We're actually older than dirt. I'm seventy-four and my husband is seventy-six."

"Thank God for Viagra," says Mr. Wasatch. "It assists the angle of the dangle."

Emanuel snickers, Leona can't help but titter, and after that things loosen up. Her husband moves his hands when he talks, florid gestures befitting an orchestra conductor, and Leona suspects he is elevating his heartbeat to stay alert. She crosses her legs, her dress glides three inches up her thigh, and the fat man's mouth forms an oval. She does not want Mr. Wasatch kneeling over her body, thinks he might hurt her if his arms give out.

"What I'm suggesting," Mr. Wasatch says, "is I don't know why we can't jump from the interview to the bedroom."

Mrs. Wasatch removes a jar of mentholated balm from her purse. "For the pulled muscles afterward."

Leona starts laughing. She doubles over and gulps huge breaths and points at the jar. Emanuel pounds her on the back but she isn't about to stop and she laughs the Wasatches and their mentholated balm out of the house and into their Cadillac. Then she laughs all the way to her bedroom, where she yanks her dress over her head and sits in cotton-shrouded silence. Out in the hall, Emanuel knocks and tells her in a loud voice next time it will go smoother.

"I don't see why you don't pick up woodworking," she says, matching volume. "I bought you all those chisels for your birthday."

Her husband has not stepped happily into retirement, misses the plant, where he was floor supervisor and responsible for turning out seventy-five ceiling fans an hour. He has tried to keep himself occupied, first by fixing every little thing that was broken around the house, then attempting a failed run at a county seat. She blames his latest obsession on a roving eye he developed on their trips to the spa, has tried to reduce her weight to the woman of her twenties, cannot keep up with the pretty young things who squeal through entire aerobic classes without breaking a sweat.

"I never should have quit," he says. "I should have worked until they forced me out the door."

The next few minutes pass without a word between them. She thinks that is that, is surprised to hear him ask if she is all right.

"I'm fine," she says.

"Okay, then."

It is not okay, not even close.

Leona finds the tape while she searches pockets prior to washing clothes, waits until she is in her room that night to turn on the cassette player. She hears an explosion. Then the crackle of gunfire, sporadic, then never ending. She pictures the jungle all around, banana leaves so broad they block sunlight.

"I'm in a muddy foxhole," Emanuel says. "I'm here and all I can think of is you."

The noise becomes so loud it is impossible to hear him and it is easy to imagine he is dead, blood gushing like a crimson waterfall out of his chest. Leona holds her breath through this part, thinks the worst possible things, so when his voice comes on again the relief is sweet as can be. Another explosion sounds. This one louder than the first.

Emanuel's voice cuts through the chaos, and he talks about coming home and starting a family. He wants two kids, doesn't care if they are boys or girls. Leona thinks that is poignant, the part about new life in the midst of all that death and destruction. She draws into herself and imagines bullets ricocheting off trees, mortar shells detonating nearby. She smells gunpowder, hears the screams, senses young men expiring around her. She tries to imagine what she would think of in Emanuel's place, if she'd worry about herself or dream of her lover.

The tape ends, and Leona unscrews the top to a perfume bottle. Rose. Her husband's favorite. She dabs the sweet scent on her wrists, tiptoes down the hall, and stops at his door. Leona yearns for the warmth of his bed, but does not have the courage to take another step in his direction. She turns and heads to her room. *Her* room. How odd the lines that now etch their lives.

Later, as the moonlight shines through the curtains and casts textured shadows across her bed, she replays the tape. Young Emanuel had loved her with a passion all the bombs in the world could not extinguish. She had loved him back.

That seems like a long time ago.

Heather shows up on the doorstep, says she needs to get away for the weekend. She wears her brown locks cut close to the scalp, a grim hairstyle she has not changed in three decades. Her dress, gray as an approaching cold front, hangs off her shoulders to her calves. Leona puts fresh sheets on the bed, goes up to the attic, and digs out a bunny rabbit. Sets it atop the dresser. Hopefully the pink will brighten her daughter's mood.

The surprise arrival has come just in time. Emanuel has lined up an interview for tomorrow afternoon, this with a couple close to their age. She must admit that riding the stationary bicycle down at the spa has done her husband good. He still sleeps more than she thinks is healthy, but he's dropped at least two pant sizes and seems lighter on his feet. Trying to do her part, Leona has started day hiking the trail, an exercise that makes her sore in the ankles and hips. She thinks, if she can become fit enough, that she might bring along a pair of pruning shears for old time's sake. Maybe she'll hide them in her day pack, snip a few briars when no one is around to make a fuss over someone her age maintaining trail.

After a dinner of vegetarian chili, Heather's favorite, Leona and her daughter sit on the porch. The night breeze pushes through the screen and brings out goose bumps on Leona's arms. She wraps a shawl around her shoulders and studies her oldest. Heather wears the same moody dress, has her head down, seems determined to while away the evening staring at her nails.

"I think your brother left Thailand and went to Iceland," Leona says.

"I found a swinger magazine when I was in the bathroom. It was under the fresh towels."

Leona draws the shawl around her neck. "I throw them away when I find them, but he's like an alcoholic hiding a bottle. You can never find them all."

Heather takes on a chiding tone. "It's one thing to talk about it and laugh over the phone, but actually seeing it is disgusting."

Her daughter's opinion surprises Leona.

"Your father and I are not prudes," she says.

Bluish light strobes out of the living room, through the sliding glass doors onto the porch, and she knows without looking Emanuel's finger incessantly taps the remote.

"Mom, do you think I'm stuffy?"

Her oldest doesn't know how to enjoy herself, an attribute she put to good use at Ohio State University, then later when she interned at Massachusetts General. Heather is in perpetual control, and Leona suspects more than a few pregnant patients appreciate her daughter's focus.

"You're a doctor," Leona says.

Heather sips her cocoa, holds the mug in both hands. The breeze changes direction and carries with it the aroma of grilled hot dogs. A balloon drifts across the yard, settles in front of the screen door, bobs on the ground as though it lacks energy to continue its journey. Her daughter's voice sounds tired and broken. "She left me, and this time it's for real. She took all her things, including the bed and the breakfront."

They talk in low tones, Heather getting it out one strained syllable at a time. Her lover has taken another, a stripper who drives a Corvette and dances around a chrome pole on an elevated stage. Heather claims the relationship won't last a week and her lover will come crawling back, but this time she is drawing a line in the sand.

"I am not a piece of shit," Heather says. "She can't come and go as she pleases."

Emanuel appears and asks how his girls are doing, walks back inside. Her husband gravitates toward his kids when they are in trouble, yet he exercises the good sense to stay clear when they talk to their mother. Appreciative, Leona pours a cup of cocoa, takes it to him, and returns to the porch.

"You really should stand up to him," Heather says. "You should stop this nonsense once and for all."

"It's not so bad. We both like to meet new people."

"Mom!"

"Now hush, we haven't actually done anything."

Heather chuckles. Unlike Parker, she barely moves when she laughs. Leona's hand seeks the warmth of her own stomach, and she marvels at how one womb can produce such different people. She gives her daughter a big hug and thinks about asking if she wants to go hiking tomorrow, nixes the idea. Heather likes to sleep in whenever she visits.

The strobing coming out of the living room stops, and Leona goes in and unfolds a blanket over her husband's lap, leaves the television on so he won't be confused when he wakes. She meets her daughter in the kitchen. In the bright light, Heather looks older than her age. Leona's stomach twists. Growing old is one thing, watching it happen to your children is something else entirely.

"I don't know what I'd do without you and Pop," Heather says.

Her daughter pads off, and Leona's heart beats a fierce rhythm. Any woman who leaves Heather is a darn fool.

Leona almost reached the ledge yesterday, which is a mile up from where the trail crosses the road, but stopped short, like a kid who puts off opening a present to prolong anticipation. She has roamed these mountains since she was young, has stood on the edge many times. Back then she walked on legs that never grew weary. Now, dressed in jeans and a long-sleeved shirt, big brown boots on her feet, she listens to her legs complain every step and satisfies herself with the knowledge reaching her goal is no small accomplishment. Her day pack holds water and a candy bar, along with a snipper she uses to cut flowers at home. She cannot move the larger branches that lie across the trail, but anything small she cuts and tosses into the weeds.

The trail, which starts out level, begins an upward slope through the hardwood forest. The air is cool, enough to tingle her ears. A pileated woodpecker swoops over the brush and latches onto a tree trunk. The bird cries its shrill sound and flies onward. Her heart skips beats if she walks too fast, so she takes measured steps and turtles along. Later in the year, when the northbound thru-hikers reach New Hampshire, this section of trail will become crowded. She thinks of the hikers down in the southern states, toiling their way north, knows the journey will be too hard for most of them and they will quit in the small towns along the way.

Her mind turns inward, and she can't help but think her life has become an uphill climb. She has a son too itchy to stay in one place, a pervert for a husband, and a daughter who returns home whenever she has lover problems. Not that Leona begrudges the intrusion. It is nice to see Heather . . . it would have been nicer under different circumstances. Leona chides herself for the thought and walks faster for punishment.

As the trail rises in elevation, spruce grows in clusters, and moss clings to outcropped rocks. Sound is muted, save for the crunch of her boots on the pebbles and the dry husk of her breathing. The change in Emanuel worries her the most, and Leona wonders if she should go along with his desire at least once. Do it, get it out of the way, move on with their lives.

The precipice appears so abruptly she almost passes it in her concentrated state. She stops and looks down into the valley, where a creek, glittering in the sunlight, meanders across a pasture and under a two-lane bridge. In the trees at the bottom of the drop off, crows caw to one another. Leona stretches her legs, sips from her Nalgene. Her cell rings, and she puts it to her ear.

"What?" Leona says. "What did you say?"

"She called and wants to get back together."

"Oh."

"Pop's taking me to the airport," Heather says.

"Now?"

"Love you, Mom!"

Leona swivels toward the direction that will soon swallow her oldest, picks out the notch on the horizon. There, a road sweeps down into a larger valley and T-bones into a highway that leads to the airport where Heather will board a jet on her way to Massachusetts. Her daughter is unlucky in love. It is not something a mother can fix.

"We've been swinging for five years," Mr. Tannenbaum says. "The time has been most enjoyable."

Leona suggests they hold the interview in the backyard, adds that black fly season isn't for another couple weeks, and the four of them head for the lawn chairs on the manicured grass. Mr. Tannenbaum's mustache is too bushy for Leona's taste, but his eyes are green and his voice is distinguished. Mrs. Tannenbaum has delicate gray hair, enviable cheekbones, and had once been beautiful. Leona glances at her blouse, checks all the buttons to make sure they are secure. Emanuel nudges her.

"Honey," he says. "They are asking if you have sexual preferences."

"I like to take it up the ass while my old man watches," Leona says.

Mrs. Tannenbaum says, "My stars."

Emanuel asks Leona to follow him to the kitchen. She does.

"Are you going crazy?" he says. "Are you off your rocker?"

Leona cuts coffee cake into four squares, licks crumbs off her fingers. "I've been reading your magazines."

"We are cultured people, we don't talk that way."

"I'm sorry," she says. "I guess I'm not myself today."

"Okay, then."

She wonders where Parker is at the moment, has the vague

suspicion she is forgetting something. Oh, the coffee cake. She slides the squares onto plates and asks Emanuel to carry two on his way out.

The afternoon temperature is comfortable, and Leona sits quietly in her chair. Conversation turns to retirement, and Mrs. Tannenbaum talks about how she volunteers in a soup kitchen in downtown Buffalo. Her husband competes in senior triathlons, had set a New York State record in the mile swim in his last event. Emanuel drops his fork, picks it up, wipes it on his napkin.

"I must ask for the recipe for this cake," Mrs. Tannenbaum says. "It's very moist and sweet."

Leona dips her finger in her tea and swirls the ice cubes.

"Moist as a juicy pussy," she says.

Feeling Emanuel's glare between her shoulder blades, she excuses herself and carries the plates to the kitchen. Mrs. Tannenbaum walks in, wets a dishrag, and dabs a spot on her dress, says it had been a long drive and they stopped for hamburgers and she spilled ketchup on her lapel.

"You needn't worry," Mrs. Tannenbaum says. "All we do is go to separate rooms and talk. It's good for their egos."

"Excuse me?"

"Nothing ever happens. We don't actually do anything."

Leona follows her guest to the yard. Nothing ever happens? She snorts her disbelief, then whispers in Emanuel's ear.

"I'm giving in," she says. "You want this, you've got it."

Emanuel clambers to his feet and suggests they retire inside. The four of them, sore from sitting, limp into the house and down the hall. Mrs. Tannenbaum and Emanuel enter his bedroom, and Mr. Tannenbaum and Leona enter hers. She sits on the bed, up near the pillow, and Mr. Tannenbaum sits next to her. He crosses and uncrosses his legs, does it again. Poor thing, he is nervous as a teenager. He smells like sweat and Aqua Velva aftershave, a musky scent that stirs her in a way she has not felt in a long time. Leona unbuttons her blouse and shrugs it over one shoulder, a pose she has seen in the movies. She feels displaced, as though the top of her head has unscrewed and the real her wriggled out and floated against the ceiling. She watches her hands shrug the blouse to her waist, watches Mr. Tannenbaum unbuckle his belt, unzip his trousers, part the opening in his boxers.

"We need to hurry," he says.

The shock of seeing him on display is like falling into an icy puddle, and she gradually returns to her body, aware of a constant knock from out in the hall. The knock grows louder, and Mrs. Tannenbaum whispers for her husband. He zips up, goes to the door, and Leona glimpses his wife peeking around his shoulder.

"She has her blouse off," Mrs. Tannenbaum hisses. She draws her husband into the hall, and Leona doesn't need to watch them leave to know they are on their way back to New York.

She stretches out on the bed, belly rising and falling, wonders how far Emanuel had gone with his date in the other room. She lifts her dress, and her fingers creep beneath her panties. Her husband has always been so careful with her, so gentle. . . .

Another knock, this one much softer, and she invites Emanuel inside. Her legs are spread and she has never felt more vulnerable, should be embarrassed, is not. His fingers take the place of hers, and he asks if this is what she wants. She says this is the only thing she *ever* wanted, then asks if Sinatra might be appropriate for the occasion. He tells her that he'll be right back, that it will only take a moment to find the right album, and sometime later she discovers him asleep in his recliner. Leona covers him to the neck with her shawl, slips off his shoes. He wakes and apologizes for getting sidetracked, holds her hand, asks her to visit him tonight. She runs her fingers through his hair, loses herself in the yellow strands, marvels at the fullness. . . . That forgetting feeling comes over her, ephemeral, elusive, like whatever she seeks floats in a mist just out of reach.

The mist clears, only for a moment, a clarity that prods her toward the phone. She has forgotten to call Heather to see if she made it safely back home to Boston. Leona dials and looks out the window at the mountains while she waits for her oldest to answer. The last remnant of the lowering sun paints the slopes a deep amber, and on the ridges fog tendrils snake out of the folds like wood smoke. She nods respectfully and sits at the breakfast nook. Leona and Emanuel Brougham are not dead yet.

5

APRIL 7TH: I drive to a used car lot and sell my Buick. The money more than pays for a shuttle up to Amicalola Falls, where the approach trail ascends to Springer Mountain. On the way out of town, I ask the driver to stop at a pay phone and I get out and call Roxie. Across the street, a woman and a fat kid sit in deck chairs next to a hotel pool. She wears a one piece, and the kid has on baggy trunks that hang to his knees. The woman shakes her finger at the kid, who unwraps a honey bun and crams it in his mouth.

Roxie says hello, and I tell her I sold my car and I'm on my way to the AT.

"Just like that?" she says.

The fat kid jumps into the shallows. Water splashes over the side, onto the woman, who closes her book and towels off her legs. The woman scoots her chair away from the pool and lies back down. My ear—the one pressed against the phone—itches, so I move the phone to the other ear and scratch away.

"I have to do this," I say.

The fat kid waddles to the deep end and dips his hand in

the water. I hope Fatso can float because the last thing I want is to fish some drowned kid out of the swimming pool. The woman looks up and says something, and the kid walks across the concrete to a trash bin and throws away the plastic wrapper. I change the phone to the other ear, listen to Roxie breathe in and out.

"I'm giving up coke for good," she says. "You, me, we'll work it out. We'll get regular jobs and move into a—"

"I want you to meet me up in Franklin, North Carolina. Twelve days from now. I got us a room reserved. It's a trail town over the Georgia border."

Her words have a bite to them. "I'll have to borrow my mom's car."

Roxie's pissed because I didn't leave her the Buick, but I know her too well. She'd drive it for a week, then sell it for a high.

"Come if you can," I say.

"I'm not saying I will, and I'm not saying I won't."

I give her directions, hang up, and watch the fat kid wade through the shallow end. He wears blow-up floaties on his arms, and he flails in tight circles. The kid takes aim at the deep end. He has this grim smile and paddles for all he's worth. His eyes are wide open, like he's scared and surprised at the same time. I know the feeling. I've lived my life on flat land, never walked through mountains. Am I scared? Hell yes. But there's no sense admitting it, no sense saying it out loud.

Normally, when I think of a shelter, I think of a building in a city where crackheads go for free meals and cot space for the night. Springer Mountain Shelter, perched on the southern terminus of the Appalachian Trail, is something altogether different. On a mountain north of Atlanta, 3,780 feet above sea level, this shelter has three walls made out of logs that intersect at the corners and rise to a slanted roof. Inside, five guys and one girl mill around. Water bottles, camp stoves, headlamps, guidebooks, boots, food bags; name it and it's scattered to hell and back. The girl wears a purple fleece and purple shorts, trail runners to match. A guy with dreadlocks lights a pipe and passes it around. An earthy smell fills the air. I stand at the edge of the shelter, under the overhang. When the pipe comes my way, I hit it and hold it out to a guy who waves it off. The guy has a bear tattoo on his neck, and he wears his hair in a black braid that falls over his shoulder and down his chest. He has flat cheekbones and wide-set black eyes. Tells me his name is Richard Nelson, and this is his first thru-hike. He opens a bottle of Crown Royal and passes it around. I sip and the liquid turns to fire in my stomach.

The girl's name is Stacy, and she watches me. Her eyes glaze over, and I don't know if that's because of the pot or if she likes what she sees. Matching silver bracelets jingle when she moves her hands. She gives me a half wave, says before I walked up they were taking turns saying why they're hiking the trail.

"I'm here to grow," Stacy says. "I'm a plant and the trail is my nourishment."

An older man, white hair frizzed around the ears, says he's getting over a divorce and he wants to live a little for the first time in his life. He says you're never too old for adventure.

"I'm a shaman," Richard says. "My people call me Waknasha-tee, which means Man Who Talks to Spirits."

"That's very cool," Stacy says.

Richard whispers in my ear. He says, "White man, if you want to get laid on the trail, you best come up with some New Age shit mixed with nature."

I hit the pipe its third time around the shelter, exhale, and zip up my fleece. There isn't much of a view—too many trees in the way—but there is a vastness beyond the forest, a wildness that settles like a cold hand on my neck. Stacy smells like cinnamon and weed, and I stare at her legs, at the fine blond hairs on her thighs.

"I bet you have a secret reason for coming out here," she says. "Something you'll never tell a soul."

"It's no big deal." I glance at Richard, who looks at me slant.

"I bet it's mysterious," she says. "I bet wild horses couldn't drag it out of you. If anyone found out you'd dry up and blow away like a tumbleweed."

"I'm a Druid," I say, and wave off the pipe. "I'm out here to sleep under oak trees and gain power from the forest. Thru-hiking the trail is a spiritual adventure."

Stacy's hand seeks mine, and warmth seeps into my skin. She clears a space next to the wall, and I unroll my ground pad and sleeping bag, light my stove and cook a dinner of Lipton noodles. The salesman tried to sell me freeze-dried meals, and I turned him down. Lipton Dinners are super-light and less than a dollar at the Dollar Store.

When it gets dark, Stacy props herself on an elbow and kisses me. I drag my sleeping bag over our heads, speak in a low voice. "My girlfriend is meeting me in North Carolina."

"No strings," she says. "Two hikers having fun."

"I'll think about it."

I don't know why I'm playing hard to get. Seriously, I'm acting like Roxie and I have a regular relationship, the kind where people say "I love you" and swear to always be true to each other. Roxie and I were never like that, even when we were living together. We had an unspoken agreement. You screw whoever you want, but you come home to me at night. Anything else was too complicated.

Stacy's hand slides under my shirt and up my stomach, and her fingers search out a nipple. Her elbow brushes my crotch and I resist the urge to push upward. I remove her hand, shift toward the wall to put a little distance between us. Turning her down feels good in a way I can't pin down.

"Are you really a Druid?" she says.

"Hell no. I don't know why I said that."

She giggles. "I knew you were full of it."

"I'm a plant?" I say. "The trail is my nourishment?"

She giggles louder. "I'm here for the party."

We quiet down and I sit up in my sleeping bag, look at moonlight shafting through the branches. A wind blows across the mountain, and tree shadows move over the ground. On the other side of the shelter, the old man mumbles in his sleep. Stacy's face, a pale oval in the darkness, turns toward me. I tell her goodnight and lie back down. I have 2,160 miles in front of me, and every step takes me further from Roxie. She better have her sweet ass in Franklin.

In prison, to pass the time, I thought about past lovers, tried to list them all and gave up when I realized my Atlanta memories were too chaotic to sort out. A redhead I met in Hawkinsville was first on the list. Suzette had this way of pursing her lips and looking at the ground like she was thinking about something important.

I was the bony kid who followed her around the playground and tapped her shoulder when she wasn't looking.

In eighth grade—this was the grade when I started jacking off—we went to her house to share homework assignments. I was good at math and she was good at history, which is the class where I fell asleep on a regular basis. We sat at the kitchen table, and I looked at the mounds under her shirt while she did word problems. I couldn't stop looking, and one day I squeezed her boobs. She bent over her notebook like there was nothing going on, so I went for it and unzipped her pants. This is around the time her mother came home from where she worked at a factory two counties over. I withdrew my finger and opened my textbook, but my mind was on the slick hole between Suzette's legs.

She told me she wanted a senior to pop her cherry, and I suppose that's what happened because there wasn't any blood when she and I snuck into an abandoned house months later and I spread my jacket over a lumpy couch and we went at it. She kept her eyes closed, like she didn't want to see what was going on. I didn't last long, hell, it was my first time. Later, when she came up to me after school, I walked in the other direction and said things like "I have to get home and help around the house."

Which was partially true. After my mother took off with that rich ex-rancher, Pop depended on me to clean house and have his dinner made when he came home from shooting pool.

The second night after she ran away, I sneaked into my parents' bedroom and cracked the window so I could hear the truck if Pop drove up. I sniffed the air, breathed in my mother's perfume, a scent that was already giving way to the mustiness of my father. The sheets were rumpled into a ball at the foot of the bed, and I suspected Pop had slept on the mattress last night. His pill bottles were lined up atop the dresser, and I cracked one of the lids and looked inside. The pills were white and large, and I studied them with all the hatred my young body could muster. I wanted to throw them away, but my father had prescriptions and there was an inexhaustible supply of narcotics at the local pharmacy. Not to mention that he would probably beat my ass.

I opened the top drawer—his socks on one side, hers on the other—fingered the soft cotton that once warmed my mother's feet. There were five drawers and I went through them one at a time. The clothes my mother had left behind were on the right and Pop's were on the left, right down to the undershirts in the bottom drawer. I wondered if it had always been this way, this separation of clothes, or if this happened recently. I straightened up and on top of the dresser, tucked inside an NRA magazine, something white caught my eye. It was a sealed envelope addressed to Pop in my mother's handwriting. I crammed the envelope in my pocket and closed all the drawers, made sure the pill bottles looked like they hadn't been moved.

Later that night, after Pop came home from the bar, he changed into shorts and a red T-shirt, came to the kitchen table when I called him for supper. He nodded off between picking at his Mac 'n' Cheese and sipping diet root beer. I tried to engage him in conversation but it was like trying to talk to someone who stood at the other end of a long tunnel, like my words traveled a million miles before they reached his ears. I asked how he did at pool and twenty minutes later he said, "All right." I told him I saw a stray dog behind Quincey's Super Market, and sixteen minutes later he said he'd look into it tomorrow. I know these times because I stared at the oven clock, watched that minute hand sweep in slow circles.

"I found a note Mom wrote," I said. "She said she was headed for greener pastures and not to look for her because she was never coming back to God-forsaken Wyoming."

The response came quickly, as though the turn in the discussion shocked Pop out of his stupor. He raised his left hand, a streak of blue chalk on his index finger, pointed straight at me. He squinted and shook his head, side-to-side, so violent it was a wonder he didn't break his neck. I'd seen him do this in the past, this desperate attempt to clear his mind during a conversation.

"You were an accident," he said.

"What?"

"It's your fault she left," he said. "She never wanted a kid and you came along and now she's gone."

The hand lowered and Pop's chin nodded toward his chest. A silver strand of drool formed at the corner of his mouth, stretched downward, and pooled on his shirt. I put his plate and glass in the sink, nudged my head under his arm, and tugged until he stood on his own. Guided him to bed and shoved him forward. He landed face down and stayed that way while I set his alarm. His words, blaming me on his failed marriage, would have crushed most boys. Not me. I knew better. Mom left because Pop was a pill popper.

Richard and I sit on a log in a clearing next to the trail. A fire ring, charred tinfoil among the ashes, forms a scraggy circle. Poplar trees tower overhead, bare branches seemingly scraping against the sky. A squirrel jumps from tree to tree, tail stretched out during the flight, lands surefooted and quick each time. The squirrel sits on a limb and peers down at us, chatters annoyance that we inhabit its universe. For a moment I feel like an outsider, like I'm trespassing on hallowed ground, but hiking the AT is my dream and I'm not about to leave it anytime soon. I stuff my fleece into my pack, buckle the top lid in place. I started six days ago, and I'm still seeing hikers I met on the first night on Springer Mountain. I've seen Stacy four or five times, talked to her while we ate lunch at a couple of shelters, but I've seen Richard the most.

A gray-haired hiker walks past, nods hello, and stumbles forward. He rights himself, curses, and stumbles again. I know the feeling. The trail is full of rocks and roots, and a lack of concentration can result in a spill and broken bones. I have fallen twice, have scraped knees to prove it, once narrowly missing a boulder that would have cracked open my skull. Another hiker walks past, younger and faster on his feet, and Richard and I return his wave.

I've been reading the shelter logbooks, trying to get a sense of who is on the trail. My guess is over a thousand hikers started in front of me. We're like this undulating human wave rolling north. There's this hiker named Simone who started calling herself Never Lost on top of Blood Mountain. I'd like to meet her and this other hiker nicknamed Buttercup. My trail name is Tazmanian Devil, and Richard's is Red Bear because of the tattoo on his neck. He's been nursing his Crown Royal and has two swallows left. He drinks them both and tucks the empty bottle in his pack.

I unwrap a piece of hard candy, suck on the raspberry flavor. Turns out Richard is from Montana and his family has an Indian gene that surfaces every half century. He's the spitting image of his grandmother; the rest of his family has blond hair and blue eyes.

"My parents are nudists," he says. "Can you believe it?"

I don't know what to say to that, so I swig from my water bottle. Peer down into it and spot a leaf on the surface. I unscrew the lid, fish out the leaf, flick it at my feet.

"A month before I started this hike," he says, "Mom and Dad got up from the supper table and took off their clothes. They took off *everything*. I'd seen Dad's swinging dick, but shit, dude, what man wants to look at his mom's you know what. I mean, I've already had one tour of that hole. They wanted me to join. Said they played volleyball, ate grilled hamburgers for lunch, and watched movies at night."

"No shit?"

"I'm not joining a nudist colony where my mom's a member. Know what I'm saying?"

I open a baggie of trail mix, eat a handful. The texture—soft raisins, hard peanuts, M&M's that melt if I hold them on my tongue—delights me and I'm already three-quarters of the way through the bag.

"I mean, there's nothing wrong with it," he says. "I could hike naked and it wouldn't bother me at all."

He takes off his shirt and pants, a pair of polka dot boxers. His skin has the tint of undercooked ham.

"You'll freeze your nuts off," I say.

"You should give it a try. It's very liberating."

He heads up the trail, a slim, naked Indian with a pack on his back. He's a fast uphill walker and ten minutes later he's out of sight. I don't try to catch him. It's hard enough walking these mountains without keeping up with some guy who has pistons in his legs, plus who wants ass in his face? Not me, that's for sure.

The climb, like the ones that came before, starts out hard and stays that way. The pitch is so steep the angle stretches my calves and in less than a hundred yards I prop myself against a tree, my chin digging into the scaly bark. I tell my body if it gets me to the top of this mountain, I'll treat it to a candy bar. It's a lie. I'm fresh out. I start again and walk through a rhododendron patch, steps so slow I'm almost in reverse. A hiker comes up behind me, and I step to the side so he can pass. Then another hiker comes, and another. A couple—a man and a woman wearing bright Dana Design packs—come up and I move over. I shake my head in disgust. I'm so out of shape I have not yet passed another hiker while going uphill. My chest heaves and my legs tingle, a sign of oxygen depletion, and I slow even more to avoid passing out.

To take my mind off the climb, I think about Roxie and what she likes and how I liked to give it to her. She has this thing about cars. One time she took me to a parking garage and got up on this black Ford while I hooked my toes under the grille and pounded away. Back then, when I was shooting coke, I could pump for hours and not get off. I swear she kept a list of exotic cars. On the list were a Mercedes, a Porsche, a silver Jaguar, and two stretch limos. That night we finished up on a Mary Kay Cadillac. Left three dents. Two from my knees and one from her ass. I don't know if the pink car made the list. Didn't care. It was her list.

Our sex was raw, the kind where a man doesn't apologize for watching a dildo go in and out of his girlfriend's pussy. That was the coke. Before I started using, sex was secretive, hurried, and I felt guilty afterward. One thing coke did for me—it got me over my guilt.

The climb is relentless, each step a strain, and I breathe so hard my chest hurts. My mind tells me to give up and go hang out on the beach until money runs out. Drink rum and coke, lie under a cabana, stop putting my body through this pain. I tell my mind to shut up and it does, and I concentrate on each gained foot of trail. An hour later I get to the peak, take off my pack, and sag against a boulder. Richard, still naked, sleeps under a tree. To the east, a hazy cloud blocks the sun. Far out, everything is so blue I can't distinguish between land and sky. I study the mountain tops, try to imagine what they looked like when first formed. The books I'd read said they rose 50,000 feet into the air, and I wonder how far a shadow something that tall could throw.

After a while, I stretch out my legs and listen to wind sigh through the trees. The rhythm reminds me of water breaking on an ocean shoreline, feels timeless in a calming sort of way. I fall asleep for a few minutes, wake up and toss a pebble that hits Richard's forehead, tell him to wake his ass up. He opens his eyes, yawns, starts a conversation about these tiny white flowers that grow in bunches close to the ground. Richard knows everything there is to know about wildflowers, says trilliums are one of his favorites and we should start seeing them in the lower elevations. He also knows about trees and animals, can identify a bird by its call. Yesterday a bird flew out of the side of the mountain close to our feet, and he parted the vegetation and pointed out a nest built into a crevice.

Now, he says, "Have you fucked her?"

"Who?"

"What do you mean 'who?'"

He's talking about Stacy, of course. I get up and put on my pack.

"Keep an eye out for the cavalry," I say. "I hear they shoot redskins these days."

"White man's got pussy climbing all over him and he doesn't know what to do with it." Richard closes his eyes and crosses his

arms, lolls his head to the side. I walk to where the trail descends
the mountain, stretch out my stride, and pick up the pace. I'm fast
as anyone on the downs. If Richard wants to keep up, he'll have
to get it in gear.

When I was nine my mother drove me south, through the desert to Rawlins, where she enrolled me in swimming lessons at
the YMCA. There wasn't a pond, lake, or river within twenty-
five miles of where we lived, so I thought if she was trying to
save me from accidental drowning, we were wasting our time.
Once a week we made the journey south in the pickup, past land
so brown and dry it only held antelope and rattlesnakes. She
dropped me in front of the huge glass doors and drove into the
city. I spent the hour squinting from the chlorine, sliding through
that cool water, my arms and legs contorted in various positions.
I learned the backstroke, the sidestroke, the Australian crawl, and
the butterfly. I learned how to rescue a drowning victim, learned
CPR and how to wet a towel and snap it so hard it left bruises on
skinny thighs and buttocks.

After class Mom picked me up and we drove around the city
before heading home. She pointed out the different things to do
in Rawlins, like going to the movies and eating in fine restau-
rants. She got a faraway look when she talked, like she would
rather live anywhere but Hawkinsville, Wyoming.

Turns out I had a body built for speed in the water and my
coach asked me to join the swim team. Mom said no, that she
had only wanted me to learn how to swim and becoming a racer
wasn't part of the deal. We stopped traveling to Rawlins, and Taz
Chavis, one hell of a swimmer according to everyone who had

seen him in the water, went back to his life in the desert. Which was fine with me. I didn't see much sense in trying to beat some guy to the other end of a pool.

As I grew older, I discovered I had attributes besides being good at swimming. Like drinking beer, huffing shoe polish, and fighting. Me and Jeffrey Lucas locked up every time we saw each other, which was at least once a day, sometimes more. I don't remember why I hated him, doesn't matter now. I'd come home with bloody knuckles, a black eye, ripped shirt or jeans, and my mother would stare at me from across the room, like I was a huge failure, this child of her loins.

The day she left she waited for Pop to leave for work, then asked me to stay home from school, said she had something important she wanted to tell me. She kept to herself in the bedroom while I watched television and ate a toasted blueberry Pop Tart, drank a soda pop to wash down the crumbs. Once I thought I heard her crying, something that had happened so often the last few months I didn't turn my head.

At 1:00—I remember the time because this was when the soap operas started, which meant nothing good was on television— she came out and sat next to me. Folded her hands on her lap. She was wearing a dress I'd never seen, a short green affair that stopped a long way from her knees. A jasmine scent filled the room.

"You have your father's blood in you," she said. "You have his blood and there's not a thing you can do about it."

A car pulled up in the driveway, and the driver honked the horn. The car was big and shiny and had a set of bull horns on the hood. My mother stood, sadness in her eyes, and looked down at me. Then she walked out the door and got in the car, and the car backed out and drove down the street. She had not told me she was leaving, had not even packed a suitcase, but she was gone for good and I knew it. A numbness I'd never felt came over me, a fog that permeated every molecule of my young body, and I stood at the window for a long time afterward. Then the fog lifted and I realized, somewhat shocked, that someone had to take care of Pop and that someone was me. That afternoon I realized my childhood was over.

Day Nine, still in Georgia, but looking forward to crossing the state line tomorrow. Richard Nelson has cut one of his shirts open around the neck and sleeves, and he wears it like a dress. NELSON TIRES is stenciled in red letters over a pocket. His family is in the tire business.

"Smell that?" he asks.

Next to the trail a spring bubbles out of the side of the mountain, forms a rivulet, and runs downhill. I dip my bottle in the water and take a cold drink. It rained last night, and water drips off glistening branches. The trail is muddy and squishy under my feet. The wind shifts, and I smell what he smells.

"Let's see what it is," he says.

"Are you crazy?"

He walks off the trail into the forest, winds his way around the mountain. I follow him through a boulder field and around an upthrust tree well that looms over my head. Brush tugs at my legs, and a thorn scrapes a thin red line on my knee. The slope steepens. I grab a boulder and haul myself along. Richard gives a low whistle and points upward.

I look where he points, and although I know what I'm seeing,

my mind takes a few seconds to register. Back in Atlanta, I saw
my share of dead guys on the street. One time I found this black
guy who'd been shot in the head. He was rolled up in a carpet
in the backseat of an abandoned car in an alley behind Frosty
Queen, and I checked on him every day to see if he was still there.
Took twelve days before the cops found him. The last couple of
days he smelled so bad I had to cover my mouth and nose.

The guy in the tree smells the same way, like someone put
meat in a cooler and left it to rot. I don't know for sure how long
he's been dead, but it's been awhile because his skin is puffy and
birds have pecked out his eyes. The side of his face has a rusted
look, like it's made of metal and has spent time in the rain. His
backpack hangs off one arm. Above him, broken branches slant
toward the forest floor.

"Probably slipped," Richard says. "See that cliff? Bet it's
right off the trail."

High on the mountain, a granite ledge merges with blue
sky. Richard climbs into the tree, shoves a stiffened leg, and the
body tilts forward. Another shove, and it falls to the ground. He
climbs down, goes through the guy's backpack, pulls out a wallet.
Thumbs through it and holds up a driver's license. "Christopher
Orringer. . . . Born in 1935."

"Old guy," I say.

"He didn't have anyone."

"What?"

"Been dead for two, maybe three weeks and there's no one out
looking for him. This guy's a goner and nobody cares."

"Got any money?" I say.

He holds up four twenties and hands me one.

"You shorted me," I say.

"I got him out of the tree."

He's right. Fair is fair.

"We should build a funeral pyre," he says. "Consider the money as exchange for labor."

"I'm not starting a forest fire."

"The woods are too wet to catch." He grabs a branch and drops it next to the dead man. "You helping or what?"

"You want my help, you give me my half."

Richard hands me another twenty, and we stack branches into a pile four feet high. He searches for a hollow log, scrapes out dry, crumbly wood from the interior, snaps twigs off a branch hanging above the ground, then builds a tepee at the bottom of the pile. He lights the wood in the center, blows on it until flame creeps upward and small branches catch fire. When the larger branches catch, we swing the man into the flames. I don't want to smell burning flesh, so I start moving through the forest. Richard catches up and leads the way, which is a good thing because I was angled in the wrong direction. We regain the trail and walk up the mountain. When we get to where the man fell, we stop for a few minutes. What looked like a cliff is actually a boulder off the trail. He must have climbed up to get a view of the surrounding mountains. We climb up and look down at smoke boiling through the trees.

"Hell of a way to die," Richard says.

I wonder what the man was thinking on the way down. Might be a bunch of bullshit but I've heard people who fall to their death relive a lifetime in a few seconds.

"You really should give Stacy a spin," Richard says. "I've seen the way she looks at you."

"I'm meeting my girlfriend in Franklin."

"Does she walk around naked?"

"You're a weird cocksucker," I say.

"I've been called worse."

Twelve days into my hike, 106 trail miles north of Springer, I arrive at Winding Stair Gap and hitch east to Franklin, where I check into the Franklin Motel and settle into my room. The air has a pine scent odor, like the maid sprayed freshener on her way out the door. The carpet is new, and the walls are freshly painted. I take a shower and wash clothes in the sink, scrub my socks three times before the water turns clear. Then I walk to the grocery store, where I buy enough food to reach Nantahala Gorge, which is less than thirty miles to the north.

On my way back, plump plastic bags dangling from both hands, I hear cars traveling highways, a barking dog, the hum of a transformer bolted to a street pole, a woman screaming at two kids in a van parked in front of the check-in office. I've lived in towns for most of my life, but this is the first time I've *listened* to one. The noise is constant, a nervous old man who can't stop jabbering.

Richard, on the sidewalk, holds up a bottle of Scotch and invites me in for a drink. I stash my groceries in my room and head his way. Inside, Stacy sits on his bed and so does Valerie, who has been in town for three days waiting for a tent manufacturer to send new poles. Valerie tells a story about a branch that fell on her tent during a windstorm, and Richard tells one about how his spirit guide, the bear, stopped him from stepping on a rattlesnake. I make one up about throwing rocks at a skunk that wouldn't get off the trail. Richard and I look at each other and a silent agreement passes between us. What happened—burning the dead guy, taking eighty dollars off him—is between us and no one else.

Valerie, a forty-six-year-old professor, takes a sabbatical every seven years and goes on an adventure. She has black eyes, a marine haircut, looks at Richard like she could swallow him whole. Stacy stares at me from where she sits on the bed. I drink what's left of my Scotch and hand my glass to Richard, who gives me a refill and hands it back. Roxie's failure to show, not even leaving a message at the front desk explaining why, only means one thing.

There is no us.

Instead of feeling sad, euphoria sweeps over me. For the first time in my life I am only looking forward. It's an airy feeling, like I've been transported to a surface with minimal gravity. I watch as Richard shrugs out of his dress and Valerie sits on his lap. Stacy sits on mine. We kiss and this time I do not move away. We leave and go to my room, where we take off our clothes and go at it. She moans and twitches, and I get into it after awhile. We screw for a half hour or so, and I roll off and stare at the ceiling. I'm breathing hard and so is she.

"How was it?" she says. "Was it okay for you?"

"Sure. . . . Sure, it was great."

I step into my shorts and walk outside. The moon, pumpkin colored and half round, suspends above the mountains. The door opens and Stacy comes across the parking lot. She's dressed, and her cheeks shimmer under the neon sign on the motel wall. I tell her goodnight and she says the same, walks down the sidewalk toward her room.

In the morning I take four aspirins to get rid of my headache, dump the food I bought yesterday into Ziploc Baggies. Richard comes in and asks if I want breakfast before we hitch to the trail. His eyes are red and I can tell I'm not the only one hungover.

"I could eat," I say.

"I'm a pancake man."

"I could eat a cow," I say.

He says Valerie was a regular cougar and asks about my night.

"We mostly talked," I say.

"I'm sorry your girlfriend didn't come."

"Ex."

"Like that?"

"Like that." My voice has a finality to it, but yesterday's euphoria over my new freedom dissipated overnight, and I'm already thinking of the letter I plan to write before I leave town.

Richard and I walk a block down the street to a diner, where I order coffee and a double order of steak and eggs. Richard orders a triple stack of pancakes and shovels it in like he's starved half to death. My seat has a rip that digs into my back, and I shift away from the aisle, settle next to the window, where I spin the saltshaker in circles. Behind a long counter a man in an apron and a white hat turns sizzling bacon with a spatula. A woman in a booth in the rear of the restaurant holds a baby to her chest and rocks back and forth. The front door opens, a squeak of metal hinges, and Stacy comes in and sits beside me.

"I'm getting off," she says. "Valerie and I are going out to New Mexico to work on a ranch and ride horses for the summer."

"Sounds good," I say.

Richard walks to the counter and pays for his breakfast, says he'll meet me at the motel. I nod, sip my coffee, cut steak into chewable pieces. The steak is medium rare, how I like it, and red juice oozes onto the plate. The coffee is hot and black.

"Valerie doesn't mind if you come," Stacy says. "The more the merrier."

"You're asking me to get off the trail?"

"You don't have to make it sound so horrible." There's a red mark on her neck, a hickey I don't remember leaving.

"I can't," I say.

"You can't or you won't?"

I drain a glass of milk, ask the waitress for another. The waitress brings the milk and I drink it down. Stacy speaks in a firm voice.

"If she loved you, she'd be here instead of me."

Although I don't look at Stacy, I feel her watching me. I finish eating, and we get up and walk to the motel, where she kisses me and gets into a rental car with Valerie and drives away.

In my room, I write Roxie and tell her I'm sorry I missed her, that I'm not ready to give up on us. I list my upcoming resupply points and estimated dates of arrival. Then I kid around and say I look forward to chocolate chip cookies in my packages. I doubt she'll send anything but it's worth a try. My hands are shaking and my body feels weak as hell. Roxie is a drug I have never been able to quit. Maybe I can walk her out of my system and maybe I can't. Time will tell.

Richard meets me at the mailbox across the street, asks if I want to carry what's left of the Scotch.

"You want it, you carry it," I say, adding there is no way in hell I'm adding the extra weight to my pack. He studies the bottle, like he weighs the pros and cons, and wistfully turns it upside down. Alcohol puddles at our feet.

"I need to lay off," he says. "I don't want to be falling off any boulders."

On the north side of Winding Stair Gap, a bird sings a three-note song. The notes have a tubular sound, a haunting that comes without warning, music that stops me in my tracks. High up, clouds ride the jet stream. The temperature is in the sixties, perfect weather for hiking this forested mountain. The pickup that dropped Richard and me at the trail head drives down the road, and he walks up the trail.

I stay where I am and watch cars speed past. I don't know what I'm waiting for or why I'm here. I think about the dead man in the forest, if the good outweighed the bad when his life flashed before his eyes. It doesn't matter, I suppose. Dead is dead.

I study a white blaze painted on the side of a tree. White blazes are the secret out here. As long as a hiker's seeing white blazes, he's on the trail. I try to think about the thousands of white blazes between Georgia and Maine, but the trail is too stretched out to imagine all at once.

6

"HON?" DALTON SAYS.

Six AM and his eyelids feel sandpapery, each scrape across his pupils a reminder he spent the night staring at the shadowed ceiling. Deirdre entwines her feet in his and issues a grumbled moan. Her nightgown smells of something he can't place. Vanilla, maybe.

"We're not getting any younger," he says. He likes looking at his wife in the mornings and rises on an elbow to study her face. Her gaze, as she drifts toward consciousness, seems innocent and pliable and reminds him of how she looked during the first years of their marriage.

"Go back to sleep," she says.

"I'll be twenty-eight next month and you're turning thirty-nine."

"I'm turning *twenty*-nine." She comes fully awake, wary gaze focused on his.

"Like I said, you'll be turning forty-nine and I'll be turning twenty-eight and it's time we started thinking about it."

"I *have* thought about it."

Dalton sits on the side of the bed and scoots his feet along the floor in search of his slippers. Barefoot, he goes to the bureau, peers into the mirror, and rubs a sleep mark off his jaw. The brush on the doily is his. The comb is hers. She cut her curls short and despite his objections will not grow them back. He raises his arms and bends at the waist. He's not as limber as he was in college, and it takes three tries before his fingers touch his toes. His cotton pajamas sag in the rear, an aggravating circumstance he mitigates with an upward jerk of the waistline.

"It's that girl," Deirdre says. She wraps the comforter around her shoulders. "Ever since she went missing you started back on this pregnancy kick."

He's always been this way. Faces on milk cartons, AMBER Alerts, anything to do with a missing child starts him thinking about what he and his wife don't have. If only she would go off the pill and let things happen. Later today, maybe he'll light a candle, turn on some easy listening, and cozy up with her on the sofa. He'll remind her, tactfully of course, that only two months ago he shut down his furniture outlet company to follow her from California to western Virginia. She's the first woman postmaster in the county, an accomplishment that pleases him. It's her turn to give a little.

"Dalton," she says. "I invited a couple for lunch."

"Today?"

"I'm sorry. I should have told you sooner."

"Not a problem." He thinks it's best to stay on her good side. "We'll talk when I get back."

On the edge of a road, on a mountain that drops to finger ridges flattening into a valley, Dalton calls for the girl, listens for a response, and hears only the trill of a distant thrush. He is amazed at how dissimilar this land is from the prosaic browns and yellows of the California desert. Here, in the belly of the Appalachians, trees have leafed out and green tints the ridges. Instead of cacti and mesquite growing out of hot sand, ferns and mushrooms populate the cool forest floor, and water trickles down narrow ravines. Chipmunks dart over logs and scuttle from hiding place to hiding place, each dash accompanied by a rustling sound. Too, the air is different, and the breeze, leftover from a recent cold snap, feels cool as a moistened washcloth against his skin.

He zips his windbreaker to the throat and thinks of the question Deirdre asked a couple days ago. He could not answer her coherently, could not tell her *exactly* why he wants a baby. It'd be nice to have a baby, he finally said. They left it at that, but last night, between beating his pillow into submission and watching the moon shadows, he started wondering if his desire to procreate is instinctual. I am, therefore I breed. Can it be that simple?

Now, he watches a forest service truck drive up, front tires bouncing across the ruts. A man in a green uniform leans out the window.

"We got a tip she's on the other side of the mountain," the man says, and sweeps his arm in a half circle.

Dalton is not surprised conversation started without exchanging names. There are no strangers when a child is lost.

"We're forming another search party this afternoon," the man says. "We could use the help."

"I can't. I have to get back home, have some things I have to do."

He slides into his sedan, waits for the truck to drive off, continues his stuttering crawl through the mountains. Stopping. Calling. Listening.

Three miles along, a fox—red tail flowing—minces through a

hemlock grove, raises its hind leg, and marks a boulder. Dalton's mind drifts away from the mountain, to a sunlit meadow. Honeysuckle scent floats in the air, and bees fat as jellybeans dart between wildflowers. Deirdre's face is turned toward the sun, and she wears a dress loosely over her mounded belly. They come to a blueberry bush and he tastes the fruit. It's sweet and juicy; a blue sky on his fingers. *The baby is kicking*, she whispers. He wraps his arms around her and moves his palm over her stomach. *We did this*, he says. *You and I. We did this—*

Whirling blades, hard chop of metal against air, and a helicopter flies over the ridge. The gravity of the search yanks him back to reality, and he is embarrassed about using the lost girl to fuel his fantasy. He gets out and calls one last time, then, remembering Deirdre's request to come home in time for lunch, turns the sedan around and drives down the mountain.

"Not now," Deirdre says, and opens the refrigerator. Although Dalton shares cooking chores—Latino-style breakfasts are his specialty—the kitchen is distinctly his wife's, and like the fox on the mountain, she marks her territory. Her notes in tiny, cursive lettering hang on every cupboard door. Things like:

SHATTER THE GLASS CEILING, SISTER.

I THINK, THEREFORE I CAN.

I AM WOMAN, HEAR ME ROAR!

The first six years of their marriage, Dalton did not begrudge this selfish tone. Only recently has he wondered if she believes her career is more important than his happiness.

"I haven't even said anything," he says. "I haven't even brought it up."

"I'm tired of it, understand?"

Her attitude needles Dalton. If anyone should be irritated, it's him. He came home early to hear lunch has been canceled, that Cloyse and Poppy Rue are coming for an afternoon visit instead. Dalton sniffs the faint odor circulating over the counter.

"Don't get mad at me," he says. "It's not my fault the tofu is getting cold."

"I'm thinking of serving chicken wings instead." Deirdre, in blouse and tights, house slippers whispering over the floor, shuts the refrigerator and clatters through the utensil drawer.

"Maybe we should open some wine?" He taps her shoulder, a boyish move that appears out of nowhere.

"Dalton."

"What?"

"I want you to promise me you'll engage in conversation." She opens the dishwasher. "Have you seen that blue bowl? The one with the gold leaves etched on the rim?"

"Are you saying I'm a stick in the mud? Because if you are, I'm not."

"I just want this to go well, okay?"

"Why don't you serve those cream cheese balls, the ones with celery and carrots on the side."

"Dalton?"

"Deirdre."

"Don't you have a brilliantly designed table in the works? Or something?"

"I'm going," he says. "You don't have to be rude."

In his study, he turns on the computer and watches a chair

revolve against a black background. Deirdre wants him to open a retail outlet in Roanoke, but he thinks he might open a woodworking shop instead, an idea that began in California, where—between sales calls, employee problems, and shuttling cheap furniture out the door at AMAZING LOW PRICES WITH NO PAYMENTS FOR THE FIRST SIX MONTHS—he spent a few minutes each day handcrafting dining room sets. The intimacy of bringing a design to life gave him a satisfaction the bulging cash register never did.

Deirdre pokes her head into the room and asks him to grab a log from the woodpile. Oak, she says, will burn longer. He waits until she leaves, shrugs into a windbreaker, and heads outside. The acre behind the ranch house has been cleared, grass planted. The woodpile is adjacent to a barbed-wire fence that runs the southern edge of the property line. On the far side of the clearing, oaks, hickories, and pines rise above ferns and form a dense forest. Above the treetops, a mountain blocks the western sky. Devoid of trees along its crown, the mountain reminds him of a balding, old man.

The window in his study opens, and he feels Deirdre's gaze on his back. A keen sound comes through the screen—steady at first—then escalating into shrieks that crash over his ears. He walks into the house, to the study where Deirdre stirs white cream in a blue bowl. The source of the screaming sits on the keyboard. The doll, a boy in sailor overalls, appeared a month into their marriage, precisely three days after Dalton brought up having a baby. Deirdre, who apparently spent a healthy sum for express delivery, named the doll Psychological Prophylactic, shortened it to PP. That first night she turned the little screamer on high and locked it in the closet so Dalton couldn't get to the control switch. The next morning, with more delight than he thought was necessary, Deirdre introduced him to each accessory, and, in less than an hour, the doll vomited a whitish liquid on Dalton's collar, defecated a gelatinous substance into a cotton diaper, and urinated a vinegary stream that splashed his forehead.

Now, Dalton's fingers find the switch between the doll's shoulder blades, and the sobbing subsides.

"Pulling out all stops?" he says.

Deirdre holds a spoon to his lips.

"Taste this," she says.

"Maybe too much basil."

"You can't hold them like that," she says.

Dalton has PP by his straw-man hair.

"It's a doll," he says.

"Do me a favor and change out of those clothes. Change into that white cardigan, okay?"

"Hear me out," he says.

"For the last time, I don't want a baby."

"I don't mind at all staying at home while you pursue your career," he says, but it is too late, she's out of the room and down the hall. He pats PP's plastic bottom. "Daddy Dalton," he says under his breath. He says it again—louder—but not so loud that she can hear it.

Cloyse Rue raises her wineglass and takes a noisy sip. The merlot has stained her lips bluish-black, a vivid contrast to her peach-colored hair. The hem of her dress settles at her knees.

Her husband, Poppy, rests his hands on his thighs and crosses his legs. Pants ride above shoelaces, expose knobby ankles encased in white socks. Poppy said, "Hello, pleased to meet you. . . . No, no thank you, I'll pass on the wine," upon arriving and has not opened his mouth since.

They—Cloyse, Poppy, and Dalton—sit in the living room, an expansive area with a high ceiling and white walls, the floor a polished hardwood. Logs crackle in the fireplace, and firelight bathes the elegant sofa and the plush recliners in an orange glow. A smoky scent hangs in the air, a leftover from when Dalton lit the kindling with the louver closed.

"More wine?" Dalton says. He's in the cardigan his wife suggested.

An eyebrow lift from Poppy, a lip curl from Cloyse, and Dalton recognizes the exchange as unspoken conversation between spouses.

Cloyse thrusts her glass forward. "I'd love s'more."

"Now, Cloyse," Poppy says.

"A teeny-weeny little more won't hurt a thing," Cloyse says.

Dalton fills her glass and excuses himself. In the kitchen, he watches Deirdre open the oven and poke a fork into a sizzling chicken wing. She wears a maroon dress, pumps to match, has on a string of pearls he purchased on one of their rare vacations. They had gone to Tahiti, where they ate seafood and lounged in cabanas during the heat of the day. Remembering how good she looked in a bikini stirs him and he comes up behind her and encircles her stomach with his arms. He rests his chin on her shoulder.

"Your friend is getting looped," he says.

"Pardon me?"

"She's an alcoholic," he says.

"She probably likes to have a good time. A little wine never hurt anyone."

"She's a bottomless pit." He nibbles her earlobe, traces the curve of her neck, tries to think of the last time they made love. It was back in California, before the move, a hurried coupling that was over as quickly as it began.

"No one's perfect," she says.

"Her husband's only here because she dragged him along. He's not engaged in the conversation at all."

"*Her* name is Cloyse and *his* is Poppy."

"I know their names, hon. I'm only wondering about the wisdom of making friends with a couple who have these kinds of marital problems."

Before she can reply, he grabs another wine bottle and heads to the living room. In California his wife only made friends with people who could help her career. Her supervisor Bob Thornfelt, a widower who bathed in English Leather before he attended dinner parties, was the most common invitee. He and Deirdre talked letters, stamps, and bubble wrap late into the night. The lead reporter for the local newspaper was also a frequent guest, and Dalton was not surprised to see Deirdre's rise through the postal service profiled in *Out and About Town*. He looks at Poppy and his knobby ankles, at Cloyse and her peachy hair—wonders how these two fit the master plan.

"I hear you're a furniture designer," Cloyse says. "That's the scoop around town anyway. You know how that is. People can be so nosy."

"I majored in ergonomics at USC."

"Mum's the word."

He swallows a yawn. "It's not really a secret."

"I need a smoke," Poppy says, and walks outside.

"Don't mind him," Cloyse says. "He's always been a party pooper."

Dalton settles into the couch and tugs his sweater over his belt. "I hear there's a search going on for a lost girl."

A *haruuumphh* comes out of Cloyse. "The last time she ran away they found her in a crack house up in Waynesboro. Like to have embarrassed her momma to death. Let's see . . . this time is the sixth time in the last two years. Folks around here don't even search for her anymore, leave it to outsiders and the law."

"I heard she got lost somewhere around—"

"She doesn't know how good she's got it. Her family's got money, loads of it. Highest producing tobacco farm in these parts." The last of her wine swirls in the bottom of the glass. He hands her the new bottle, and she pours her own.

"So," she says, "Deirdre tells me you're thinking of adopting."

"What?"

She hands him a business card. "My fee is listed on the—"

"I'll be right back," he says.

In the kitchen, Deirdre arranges chicken wings on a silver plate. The wings form a perfect circle—an inch of separation—meaty ends flared toward the edge. In the center she places a bowl filled with cheese dip. She has a deft touch, a concentrated air; attributes honed by dropping mail into thousands of slots throughout the years. Dalton wishes she would apply the same attentiveness to their marriage. Doubts she will. Theirs is an unequal love, and he is certain his is greater than hers. He measures the difference in frustration. His, of course.

"I know why you invited them," he says, when he can no longer hold it in. "Or more precisely, *her*. I know why *she's* here."

"Grab those napkins, will you? No, not the plain ones. Bring the ones with the little flowers. There, bring those." She wipes her hands on a dishtowel.

"She runs an adoption agency."

Deirdre speaks in a low, but firm voice. "I know what she does for a living."

"You *know*?"

"I asked her to come over and talk to us. Show us some four-year-olds."

"You did *what*?"

"It's a compromise, Dalton. I've been very clear about not wanting a baby."

"Don't you think you should have *asked* first?"

"You would have said no."

Deirdre picks up the platter, and he follows her into the living room. She sets the platter in front of Cloyse, who nibbles a wing and comments on the tenderness. He and his wife sit side by side on the sofa, and she takes his hand in hers. She has a warm, soft palm, and her thumb brushes his, an unspoken plea for him to at least consider possibilities.

"Please forgive the lack of political correctness," Cloyse says, "but young white children are very hard to come by these days. It's much easier to adopt a child from overseas. Asian, especially."

Dalton removes his hand from his wife's grasp, flicks his fingernail against his wineglass, and a *ping* swells through the room. Adopt? What an idiotic idea. He goes to the fireplace and throws a log on the flames. Poppy, framed in the living room window, lights a cigarette.

"Your husband smokes like a chimney," Dalton says. "He hasn't stopped puffing since he stepped outside."

"Hubby gets nervous around strangers," Cloyse says.

A sob from the rear of the house, a hiccup, a whimper, and another sob.

"You didn't tell me you were already a momma!" Cloyse says, and pats Deirdre's knee. "I got two myself. Is that a boy—"

Dalton says, "Don't get up, hon. Lord knows you've done enough today," and to Cloyse, "All he does is cry. I'd put him in the garbage disposal if Deirdre would let me. Chew his little butt right up."

"Dalton's a big kidder," Deirdre says. "He's a softy at heart."

Halfway out of the room, Dalton says over his shoulder, "The booger eater took his first steps last week. Can you believe it? Where does the time fly?"

In the study he turns the doll over, jiggles the control switch, and the sobbing morphs into a scream. He thumps PP's button nose.

"Hey, quiet down will you."

He unbuttons the sailor suit and flops the doll on its stomach. The directions begin at the shoulders and in crisp sentences work their way to the buttocks. The study door opens and Deirdre strides across the room. He shouts in her ear that he must have accidentally set the timer this morning, that the directions indicate the crying will stop when the doll is good and ready. She grabs the doll and slams it against the chair.

"Fa-rigg," she says. "Make it shut up."

"Wait, I read something that might work. Hold it against your shoulder and bounce up and down."

"I'm not sure I'm doing it right," she says.

"Slower, I think. It has to be the right rhythm."

He studies his wife, the doll in her arms, plastic chin in the hollow of her throat.

"It's working," she says.

"Hon," he says. "Look at you. . . ."

There is moisture on her pupils, a shine he rarely sees. Deirdre closes her eyes, opens them, hands him the doll. "There's an opening coming up in the district—"

"What?"

"I want more, Dalton. I want the top of my profession."

"We're talking about a two-month pregnancy leave! You're saying you can't leave your job for sixty days?" He smooths the doll's hair, straightens the crooked collar, tries not to look at that cute stubby nose.

"I told you from day one I was never having a baby," his wife says. "From day one."

PP starts up again, a startling shriek, and Deirdre walks out of the room. She looks over her shoulder to see if he is coming.

Outside, the air smells of wood smoke, and on the next ridge over, a lazy curl that hooks into the mountain, a hound begins a plaintive howl. Dalton raises a shovel and brings it down hard. The spade glances off a leg, strikes stone, and sparks shoot into the air. He swings again—the sobbing at his feet now a scream—and the spade bounces off an arm. He swings the shovel in wide arcs, and with each blow mentally rescans manufacturer catchphrases etched into the doll's back:

BUILT TO LAST.

HIGH-IMPACT PLASTIC.

LIFETIME WARRANTY.

"Hey!" Poppy runs across the yard with fists raised. "Hey! Hey! What are you doing?"

Dalton gets in one last swing and drops the shovel. His chest heaves. Poppy toes the doll, nudges a leg cocked at an awkward angle. "Shoot, I thought this thing was real. . . . What a set of lungs."

"It won't shut up," Dalton says, catching his breath.

"Why don't you just bury it?" Poppy picks up the shovel and says something about Californians being a real piece of work. "Any place in particular?"

"I'm sorry?"

"It's your yard, where do you want the hole?"

"It doesn't matter," Dalton says. "So long as it's deep."

"They found her up on the Appalachian Trail?" Cloyse says, and sips her wine.

Poppy, cell phone to his ear, covers the mouthpiece. "At the bottom of a cliff. Been dead for several days."

"I'll be," Cloyse says.

Deirdre acknowledges the news with a nod, flips open a glossy adoption catalog, and points out a boy on a rocking horse. "Isn't he the cutest thing?"

Dalton is not surprised the news fails to faze Deirdre. His wife rarely loses focus. He, on the other hand, will not allow himself to feel one way or the other about the girl. Deirdre's stubbornness makes him angry, and it's a feeling he wants to hold on to.

"That is the ugliest kid I've ever seen," he says.

His wife has a loopy smile, gooey gaze to match, and she flips pages without looking up. She points out a curly-haired girl, fingertip on the girl's foot, and Dalton calls attention to the flapjack ears and bulbous nose.

"I don't want a kid that looks like she belongs in a freak show. There, see that? The one on the bottom of the page? Check out that chin. Looks like it's been run over by a truck."

Cloyse speaks in a soft voice. "Adoption isn't for everyone; perhaps you two would like to reconsider?"

"Yes," Dalton says. "Perhaps we would."

The flashlight beam swings through the darkness, illuminating the trees, the boulders, the grass. Poppy and Cloyse are gone, fire long dead, wood smoke a memory. The chilled air is without breeze, and somewhere on the mountain the hound still howls.

Dalton tilts the beam so it shines on the freshly turned mound. The grave is long as a breadbox, and he thinks of the doll, dirt pressing on all sides, wonders if Poppy buried it right-side up. Deirdre bows her head and asks him to turn off the light. He does. He can no longer see her, but she is so close he can hear her breathing. Dalton moves toward her, a subtle sidestep that brings their shoulders together. She's trembling, and so is he.

"I feel bad about that girl," he says.

"Me too."

"Her parents must be horrified."

"People make it through," she says.

"Yes, I guess they do." He looks through the trees for the mountain, listens for the hound. Behind the branches, the peak shimmers in the moonlight.

"I don't want you to leave me," Deirdre says.

They stand in silence until she says she's going inside. He tells her he'll just be a minute, almost suggests she get out the catalog. He listens to her steps fade into the night, wanting, for a reason he can't identify, to hear the rear door open and close before he follows her down the grassy slope.

7

THE TRAIL IS nothing like I imagined. I'm a thousand miles from Springer, and the exhaustion I felt hiking over those Georgia mountains is long gone. I'm in shape, can hold a conversation going uphill and never lose my breath, but the pain never ends. First to arrive were the blisters, opened up by walking in wet shoes through North Carolina and Tennessee. The blisters healed, then my waist belt began digging into my hips. I purchased buffer pads at a hardware store to solve that problem, then pulled an Achilles tendon on The Priest in Virginia. My ibuprofen intake increased to 3,000 milligrams a day until the pain went away, and my limp swung into a normal gait.

Now I have plantar fasciitis in my right foot, and every step feels like a nail penetrates my heel. I eat ibuprofen from the time I get up until the time I go to bed. My stomach feels raw. Like a rat claws and chews at the lining, always hungry, a perpetual feeling of devouring myself from the inside out.

*　　*　　*

Day Seventy-five of my hike, I limp out of the forest and walk across a gravel parking lot. On an overlook, a man strapped under a hang glider runs to the edge and launches into open space. Fluorescent-yellow fabric snaps against the breeze. He circles on the thermal, sails into the valley and out of sight. I'm in Maryland, almost in Pennsylvania, and can see into both states, a vista of small towns with roads that run like gray arteries between fields. I've walked through leafy green forest for what seems like forever, and the sudden expanse has a magnetic feeling. I don't want to leave, but if I stop too long my foot will seize up. I tighten my load-lifter straps and my pack shifts toward my back.

"Want a beer?" a voice says.

A guy and a girl lean against a white Chevy. I limp in their direction and take the bottle, drain it, then drink another.

"Damn," I say.

The guy has close-cropped hair, like he is in the military. The girl wears jeans and a violet blouse and has that casual air of standing in her element. I thank them and tell them about my hike, like how much my pack weighs and what kind of food I eat, how far I've hiked and how long I've been on the trail—typical conversation between thru-hikers and the people we meet along the way.

Fay's teeth show when she smiles. Randy is her man, and they have the weekend off. They work for a seat cushion factory, Fay on the line, Randy in shipping.

"Randy is the best forklift driver in the company," Fay says.

Fay and Randy hold hands and drink beer. I shift most of my weight to my left foot and drink with them.

"We come up for the sunsets," Randy says.

Fay says, "One of the best views around."

I drink another beer, this one a micro brew out of Boston, and it goes down good as the first. They seem to understand trail deprivation, how much small pleasures mean to a hiker. They offer me another beer but it will get dark soon and I want to get down the mountain and pitch my tent while it's still daylight. I thank them and step into the forest. I feel good inside.

Pen Mar Park, an hour's walk from the overlook, closes to the public at sundown. There are bathrooms and running water, soda and snack machines, picnic tables, asphalt footpaths, people sitting in fields on blankets in the sun. I feel ill-placed in my dirty hiker shirt and shorts, my once-white trail runners now the color of mud, a backpack that looks like it's been run over multiple times, but hikers are a common sight here, and no one gives me a second look. I buy a Coke and salted peanuts, nod at two boys playing Frisbee, head to a grassy spot, and pitch next to Richard's tent. Another tent sits thirty yards away, backed up to a forest on the north edge of the park. Simone, or Never Lost, as she's known on the trail, sits outside the tent and dumps out her food bag. She started her thru-hike well before me, twisted a knee climbing over boulders in the Shenandoah and took time off, or I never would have caught up with her. I've talked to her a few times, ate lunch with her next to a spring, don't know her very well. She never takes a break on the overlooks. Trail rumor has it she's scared of heights.

Simone heads my way, barefoot, tells me Richard walked to the grocery store to resupply. She says she got here around noon and went into town to read up about plantar fasciitis in the library.

"The best thing is to get off your foot until the swelling goes down," she says. "Alternate heat and ice."

Stopping to rehabilitate is a bad idea. I'd grow accustomed to the easy life, and I'd get off the trail for good. I miss the showers the most.

I swallow four ibuprofen. Wash them down with Coke.

"Or," she says, "you can do this exercise called Downward Facing Dog."

"Whoof."

"Seriously," she says.

Simone has a somber face, a professorial look that dimples when she smiles. She is only mildly attractive, but she has the glow of the exceedingly fit, a sexiness so ingrained it seems to ooze from her pores. She kneels, places her hands on the ground, then her ass lifts into the air, rocks back until her heels press against the grass. Her skin is toned and without blemishes, her legs limber and strong, and it is all I can do to keep my hands to myself. I get down beside her. We do Downward Facing Dog and at first the pain in my heel hurts so much I want to stop. I keep at it, and the pain subsides.

Simone going into town to get information on my foot problem is my second kindness today. I think about the couple on the overlook, realize I have not heard their car travel the road that winds down the mountain and skirts the park. No doubt they are watching the sunset. I ask Simone to do the same and we sit in a pavilion, under a sky that reddens along the horizon. Clouds turn violet, an interlocking of lace that fades to pale orange. A purple hue takes over the heavens, and one last sun-shot cloud remains, a bright island in a darkening sea. This sunset is the most beautiful thing I have seen in my entire life. I am peaceful inside, something

I *never* was in civilization, and I'm not sure why. Sometimes I feel like I came to the trail in pieces, and the AT is reconstructing me one step at a time. At first, I thought the drumbeat of footsteps that permeate my consciousness each day, and the meditation that inevitably follows, was the source for this change, but now, sitting next to Simone and watching the sky colors fade into each other, I think maybe nature's raw, uncensored beauty has healing powers.

"A mineral spring for the soul," I muse.

"Excuse me?"

"Never mind, just thinking aloud," I say.

Simone takes a picture, shifts toward me and our legs touch. The sensation of skin on skin sends a jolt through me that I have not felt in a while. I don't want to move, but my stomach is about to cave in on itself, so I light my stove and cook cheese-filled bowtie pasta, spoon in peanut butter and hot sauce, taste, add salt and pepper. This meal is my trail specialty, and I hold out a spoonful. Simone tastes and grimaces, spits over the railing.

"I hope you don't cook for a living," she says.

"It's a cultivated taste."

I taste the sauce, dump in more salt. Retaste.

"Try again?" I say.

She shakes her head and laughs. I fail to see the humor, eat my supper in silence, get out oatmeal cookies Roxie mailed to my last town stop. Simone reluctantly bites into one, gives me a surprised look, and we eat until the Baggie is empty.

"Good cookies," she says.

"Thanks."

I don't tell Simone where the cookies came from, see no sense elaborating on how Roxie got my letter and started mailing me food. She quit coke, she says, cold turkey. Writes incessantly about how I have inspired her to lead a better life. She wants to drive up and visit, to see how we are together with our heads on straight, to test the waters, so to speak. I have a hard time believing she has changed and have not given her the go ahead.

Simone has that look women get when they want to be kissed, and my lips seek hers. The sun is all but down and we kiss until dark, and then I slide my hand between her legs. I can feel her heat and know she can feel mine. She scoots away until there is a two-foot gap between us.

"Not in town," she says. "In town we're just friends."

"We're not in a town." Technically, I think I'm right. The park butts up to a town.

"That's the deal. Take it or leave it."

Back when Roxie and I were together, she got this idea we could give up coke if we went on a three-day drunk. She believed we would wake up on day four with a bad hangover but we would be drug free. We bought six quarts of vodka at the liquor store, five gallons of orange juice from Save-A-Lot, rented a motel room, and hung a DO NOT DISTURB sign on the door. The first day we drank and watched *Seinfeld* reruns, fucked on top of this bedspread green as her eyes, beat on the wall when the neighbor hollered we were playing the television too loud. On the second day she walked to her favorite street corner and made two hundred dollars in two hours. We spent the next two days shooting coke and drinking.

A couple months later she wanted to try something else and I said sure, I'd tie her up until the craving left her body. We had plans. First she'd get clean, and then she'd tie me up and I'd get clean. I brought along a Popsicle stick for her to bite on if she got the urge to scream. She had an eight-ball, and we shot it up until it was gone. I went out and bought an ounce, cut it with baby laxative, broke it down, and sold the shit at a crack house down on Harvey Avenue. We spent half of what I made on coke, shot it up, and I kept right on dealing.

Roxie is a stone-cold junkie, and I'd have to see it to believe she quit. *Anything* is possible. I study Simone's silhouette in the twilight, the curve of her breasts under her shirt. It's cooled off between us.

Least for now.

Later that night, the park now devoid of the public, Richard lurches out of the dark and falls against a garbage can. Thru-hikers are allowed to camp if they are discreet, which Richard is not, even when he's sober. He smells like whiskey and vomit, and his lips don't work well enough for him to form understandable words. I lead him to his tent, unzip the fly, and he crawls inside. Simone comes up, and we stand around in the dark. I try to kiss her again and she balls up her fist and digs her knuckles into my chest, not so much that they hurt but enough so I know they are there. I have not fucked anyone since Stacy back in Franklin, North Carolina.

"He's thinking about quitting," I say. . . . . "He's been getting worse but says he's going to stop any day now."

Simone launches into a rant about how once a drunk always a drunk. She tells me about a book she studied in college and how the author theorized we are all born with a flawed gene that leads to our demise. I remember my mother's words when she was talking about my father—and how she thought his weakness etched my future.

"Hand-me-down blood," I say.

She speaks in a firm voice.

"From the time our father's sperm meets our mother's egg, we are who we are. Fighting it is a waste of energy."

"People can change."

Her voice, when it comes, has lost its firmness. She sounds hopeless, like she's in a dark room and can't find her way out.

"No," she says. "They can't."

"You sound like you're talking from personal experience."

She doesn't say anything, and I wish I could see her eyes, but it's too dark for that and I can only read her posture. She is tense, withdrawn, and I sense I have overstepped a boundary. The silence becomes uncomfortable and to fill it I start talking about my father and his pill habit. I tell her almost everything, leave out the part about him committing suicide. How he died is no one's business but mine.

"He started wetting the bed at night," I say. "I used to get up every morning and throw his sheets in the washer before I went to school. Then I'd come home and put them in the drier."

Simone is quiet, head cocked my way, as though she listens intently, and I continue my story, right up to me leaving that day in Hawkinsville.

"Do you feel guilty?" she says.

"I took him to NA meetings. I fed him. I got him up in the morning. I took care of him for years."

"Yes, but you still left him."

A car engine sounds up on the mountain, and I turn away and

look up the road, wanting any excuse to end the conversation. Rpms rev and the car, headlights on, comes out of the forest, down the road, at a high speed. I will the car to slow, only it is going too fast, and the squealing brakes have no effect. The car fishtails and leaves the road. Impacts a telephone pole nose first. Metal shrieks and folds inward, glass shatters, and Fay and Randy fly headfirst through the windshield. Watching them tumble, the car's rear end settling back down to the road, a hubcap rolling across the white line and into the ditch, seems so out of place for someone who has been hiking in the woods that nothing seems real. But when it is over, Fay prone in the grass and Randy across the hood, I know it is real, and along with that comes the feeling there's not a damn thing I can do about it.

Simone and I run to the car and look at Randy, at the sliver that splintered off the pole and drove itself deep into his eye. I don't check for a pulse.

The street light overhead vibrates from the impact, and the shivery light that falls over the car seems dim and impermanent. Simone has a strange smile that goes away soon as she realizes I'm looking at her. Lights blink on in a house up the street, and a man opens the front door and hollers that he called an ambulance. Simone brings her face close to Randy's. Presses her lips against his. A tender kiss, her hand on his cheek like they are lovers with a future. I have never seen anyone kiss the dead and look away like this is a private moment between family members. Then I check on Fay, whose neck twists at an odd angle to her shoulders. Simone and I stare at the body. She bends down and kisses her too.

"They loved each other," I say.

Two dead kids, a sadness, a futile feeling that I suspect Simone and I both share, a helplessness that drives us across the street, into the park, where we sit on a picnic table and watch the emergency crews arrive. An ambulance strobe brightens the night. We sit hip to hip. Stay that way until the wrecker winches the car onto the flatbed and drives down the road and out of sight. The light high on the pole is still on, and on the street glass winks under the reflection.

I have a definite sense of us and them, of the separation between the real world and the life of a thru-hiker, yet that distinction is anything but comforting. Simone and I walk to Richard's tent and stand in the spots we were in when the wreck happened. Like we're trying to rewind time. She asks if my father is still alive, and I tell her he's dead. She offers her condolences, then says goodnight, and crawls into her tent. Richard snores drunkenly, a wretched sound, the death rattle of the living, and I pull up my own tent and pitch it far away so I don't have to listen.

That night I think about the dead and how they are gone forever. Fay and Randy will never again walk this earth and neither will my father. Do I feel guilty about leaving him? A small part of me feels that way, I guess, but the rest of me is just sad. He was my father, and you only get one of those in life.

8

IN A SNIT over Pike's choice of color for the downstairs bathroom, Giuseppe says good riddance and moves out of the B&B into the garden. Instead of digging in the weeds in the shadow of the tall poplar, a patch he and Pike save for fall cabbage planting, Giuseppe plunges a shovel into a tilled row and scoops out dirt, worms, and broccoli plants. He digs toward the tomatoes, yanks an Early Girl upward, tosses it into the corn. The uprooted plant falls through the leaves and topples slowly onto its side. He slaps his palms together, a satisfactory pop filling out an otherwise still morning, sniffs the coffee smell wafting out of an open kitchen window. The property's epicenter is a two-story Victorian, white with tin roof, shutters blue as the mid-morning sky. On the far end of a sprawling lawn, Appalachian Trail thruhikers pitch their tents on ten-dollar-a-night campsites. Giuseppe wishes the hikers stayed elsewhere—more trouble for him is the way he sees it—but they spice up the ambiance, and regular guests, gay professionals from surrounding cities, enjoy the company.

Giuseppe bends to his work, and after two hours of steady

digging, widens the hole into a smooth-sided hollow. He sculpts a crumbly pillow on one end, a gritty table on the other, flings the shovel into the air and watches it stick point down in the grass halfway between house and garden. He doubts Pike, the original literal man, will understand the symbolism.

The rear door opens . . . closes on a set of raspy hinges Giuseppe should have oiled months ago. He crouches on his haunches and watches his lover walk through the garden carrying a plate of blueberry muffins. All arms and legs, head bobbing to an arrhythmical gait, Pike exudes an innocent awkwardness, and the impression of those meeting him for the first time is docile ineptitude. A false assumption. Pike is a retired attorney, a raider who dismantled companies with all the abandon of a child playing in the sandbox.

"I brought you breakfast." Pike places the plate on the ground. He wears a robe the color of his eyes—butterscotch brown—an iris tint that causes Giuseppe to speak in sentences that end in the middle of nowhere. He forces his gaze on Pike's legs, at the scar below his left knee, a wound he received in a minor car accident a few years back. Giuseppe knows every inch of that body— moles, blemishes, arthritic knuckles, how the aging spine, once so straight, bows between the shoulders—he knows it all.

Pike steps close to the hole and soil falls over the edge and puddles at the bottom. "I can't believe you are so riled up. Over such a little thing."

"I've told you before, chartreuse nauseates me. I cannot abide the idea of sitting on the toilet surrounded by puke-green walls."

Two women come outside and adjust their floppy hats and look toward the garden. It's Monday morning in Kent, Connecticut, and it's time for Wendy and Josselyn to leave the mountains and head to Boston. Pike's good-bye hugs are a B&B tradition, and he turns and walks toward the women. Giuseppe recedes into the hole. His world has shrunk to a dirt floor, four walls, a blue rectangle overhead. He paws the edge until his fingers grasp the muffin plate. One thing about Pike, the man can cook.

Giuseppe eats the last muffin and works his mouth for saliva, wonders if Pike forgot to bring something to drink on purpose. Probably so. Anything to get Giuseppe out of the hole. The sun climbs a high arc and slips behind a thin cloud layer. He stretches out his tightening back, coils and uncoils his fingers, and wishes he were thirty years younger, still sporting a ridged abdomen and the accompanying youthful impudence. Pike prefers lovers on the younger side, that's no secret, and Giuseppe shows wear, wrinkles that look like ditches when light hits his forehead just right. He's dyed his hair, camouflaged gray threads above his temples, but has been unable to avoid the feeling he's deteriorating one cell at a time.

That afternoon Pike places a pitcher on the porch rail. The setting sun illuminates the water and ice cubes swirl in amber light. Pike the temptress, Giuseppe thinks, the corporate pirate who offers drink while secretly plotting to cut your throat.

"I'd rather dry up and blow away than drink your water," Giuseppe yells, and instantly regrets his outburst. He has spent many evenings listening to Pike explain the ins and outs of negotiating. The secret is to never let them see you scratch . . . even if your ass itches so bad you can't stand it.

*　　　*　　　*

The afternoon recedes into dusk, dusk into darkness. Lights switch on inside the Victorian and shadows move across curtained windows. Doors open and close, laughter and muffled conversation escape the guests on the porch. The moon is out, an orange splash above a tendriled cloud, and stars track the sky. Tents light up like glowing orbs.

Giuseppe yells an obscenity, grins through dry lips. He yells again, a "goddamn" that ends louder than it started. Pike's voice flows through the darkness, a quiet apology to the guests and a request that everyone spend their night inside. In the next hour, windows darken one by one, and when the last light blinks out, Giuseppe screams "asshole" nine times in a row, catches his breath, screams another ten.

The rear door opens, followed by the squeak of a turning valve and the rush of water through a hose. The sprinkler sweeps over the garden, rattles the broadleafed squash and what's left of the tomato plants. Spray hits Giuseppe's face and he opens his mouth and sticks out his tongue, licks moisture from his lips.

"Are you there?" Giuseppe says, seeing only shadows at the rear of the house.

"I'm here."

The sprinkler comes around again, and Giuseppe takes the spray on his back. "I'm not saying I don't appreciate the water, I truly do—"

"I hired a houseboy," Pike says.

"How young?" Giuseppe, eight years younger than Pike's sixty, feels eighty at the moment.

"Younger than you."

They are quiet for a long time, and Giuseppe feels such an

emptiness it's like his blood has drained from his body. "You still there?"

After what seems forever, Pike's voice comes through the night. "I'm still here."

"I wish you wouldn't've done that. We really don't need a houseboy."

"It's only until you come to your senses."

The sprinkler stops, the rear door opens and closes, and Giuseppe removes his clothes and wipes water off his face. The breeze chills his slicked skin, and he wraps his shivering arms around his torso. He and Pike have been together for thirty-two years, met outside a Hartford convenience store where Giuseppe panhandled for his supper. Back then he lived in an abandoned car on a dead-end street, rummaged through Dumpsters when panhandling didn't pay off. After a brief courtship, mostly sex in the backseat of a leased Cadillac, Pike said he had room for two in his bed and Giuseppe took his offer. In the ensuing years, they lived in a series of rentals that grew pricier and higher off the ground as Pike advanced in a downtown firm. Because they were queers before queers were fashionable, they never ate in a restaurant together, never sat side by side in a theater, never went to the firm's Christmas parties. Whenever they packed up and moved from apartment to apartment, Giuseppe felt like they were starting anew and suggested they adopt a pet. He didn't care if it was a bird or a slab-sided iguana, as long as it required shared written commitment. Each time Pike said no.

Giuseppe blamed the corporate life for his lover's reticence, believed desire to get somewhere enticed ladder climbers to seek unfettered relationships. At times, he felt like a trinket so cheap Pike wouldn't hesitate to toss it in the garbage. The affairs started when Pike turned forty, voices calling in the middle of the night, hanging up when Giuseppe answered the phone, but he dug his heels in and refused to turn his lover loose. To his amazement— he couldn't believe they had been together that long—Pike retired and started shopping for a B&B. Giuseppe dreamed about the contract, imagined how they would sit around a mahogany desk and sip champagne, contract spread like a tantalizing siren across the glossy surface. He dreamed of the pen in his hand, of broad strokes on the bottom line—Pike Orwell and Giuseppe Stephanopoulos—tying the knot forever. Never happened. Pike purchased the house alone, and Giuseppe moved in without arguing the point.

Now, he faces the moon, a yellow eye that peers down at him with a reproachful stare. Giuseppe thinks he might be too hard on Pike. It isn't easy managing the B&B. Pike writes and places advertisements in niche magazines, does the accounting and taxes, designs and cooks gourmet meals. He handles the customers, makes them feel comfortable coming and going. Giuseppe washes linen and makes up the beds. He also mows, but he enjoys riding the John Deere and doesn't count that as work. They share the gardening.

Giuseppe stands fully erect, not an easy thing after moving so much dirt, and howls a mournful sound. Pike isn't the only one who can up the ante. Tomorrow, if Giuseppe can work it into the conversation, he will ask to put his name on the title.

"Joining us for breakfast?" Pike says, and motions toward the dining room table. He's in his brown robe, sash knotted below his belly button.

Mudcaked and unclothed in the hallway, Giuseppe raises a foot and scrapes the adjacent ankle with his big toe. He likes mornings in the B&B, the way house and guests wake up together, neither in a rush to greet the day. A toilet flushes upstairs, and lazy footsteps sound on the ceiling. "I wouldn't want to be a bother."

"No trouble," Pike says. "I'll set another plate and—"

"I just came in to get a few things, maybe a book and an umbrella."

"The umbrella is a good idea. The weatherman said it's going to be a scorcher today. Much hotter than yesterday."

"I was thinking about reading a little Cheever."

"You can't go wrong with Cheever," Pike says.

Giuseppe follows Pike to the kitchen and watches him flip batter that bubbles in the skillet on the stove. The pancake somersaults and lands dead center. For years Pike has performed this trick to entertain Giuseppe, who always reciprocated with an appropriately awed sound. Today he holds his tongue. Pike cuts him a glance and Giuseppe looks away.

A frail boy pads into the kitchen, pecks Pike on the cheek, opens the refrigerator, and comes away with a carton of orange juice. The boy wears tattered shorts and shirt, bandanna tied in a scarf over yellow hair. He has a lean face, sores on his cheeks— most likely, Giuseppe thinks—the worst case of acne on a scarecrow he's ever seen.

"Say hello to Dobbs Amherst," Pike says, "our new houseboy."

"I'm only staying for the summer." Dobbs opens the carton and takes an enthusiastic swallow. Giuseppe extends his hand and the boy reciprocates. His handshake is limp and unimpressive, his expression impassive.

"He just got word he's been accepted at Dartmouth," Pike

says. "He won't be able to finish his thru-hike so he's stopping here to earn play money for his first semester."

Giuseppe presses his fingertip, a grubby spear point, against the boy's chest. He pushes Dobbs against the wall, then walks outside to the black gash in the green garden, where he deposits himself with an abrupt sinking of the legs. He bakes in the heat, curses his cowardice.

Later that day, as the sun begins a downward slide, Dobbs comes out and hands Giuseppe an apple, gallon jug of ice water, umbrella, and a novel, *Falconer*, one of Cheever's best.

"Pike told me to bring you this stuff," Dobbs says. "He said you enjoy a late lunch."

Giuseppe arranges the items on the dirt table, pops open the umbrella, and stands in its shadow. His shoulders cool, and, wanting to quench his thirst, he fumbles with the jug. The boy jumps in the hole, unscrews the lid, and climbs back out. Giuseppe drinks long and hard. Between guzzles he eats the apple to the core.

"Compost," Giuseppe says, and tosses the core over his shoulder.

"Huh?"

"Never mind . . . you don't know much about gardening, do you?"

The boy tugs at the yellow wisps over his ears, and his voice grows defensive. "Least I don't live in a hole in the ground."

"It's quite comfortable, actually." Giuseppe lies on his back and looks up at the boy, whose face looks vaguely familiar from this angle.

"Do we know each other?" Giuseppe says.

"I'm Dobbs. We met about four hours ago."

"No, I mean before. Have you come through here before?" It's not unusual for thru-hikers to walk the Appalachian Trail multiple times. Giuseppe thinks they waste their lives isolated for such long periods but keeps his opinion to himself. He has no pedestal to mount while he sits in judgment. He is a house bitch, not exactly a respected station in life.

"I might have come through here," Dobbs says. "You never know about me. I get around."

"I'll bet."

"You don't have to be an asshole. I never done anything to you."

"I never *did* anything to you. Pike won't tolerate anything less than perfect grammar. He's a stickler about it."

The boy clutches a wilted tomato plant and breaks off leaves one at a time. "You'll like me when you get to know me. If you can get that fat dick up, I'll give you the best blow job on the East Coast."

"Don't you worry about what's between my legs." Giuseppe suddenly feels naked, an awareness that makes him reach for his clothes.

"A man with a cock as pretty as that one should get some love once in a while. God knows that old man in there isn't doing it for you."

"He's confused." Giuseppe steps into his underwear, tugs on the filthy cotton.

"I grew up with an uncle like him; bastard had me sucking dick when I was nine. I wouldn't even be a homo if it weren't for him. I'd be eating pussy and squeezing boobs like a normal guy."

"Pike isn't like your uncle."

"No?" Dobbs asks.

"He's a good man."

"Pike says you're eccentric, he says one time he came home from a big case and found his entire bedroom set on the street. Said cars were honking and people were stealing pillows. He said to watch out for you because you're unpredictable."

A car comes down the lane in front of the B&B, parks in the shaded lot out front. Giuseppe doesn't need to look at the plates to know they are government issue. A man gets out and strides across the yard to the tents. The state police. They've been regular visitors ever since a Boy Scout went missing on the trail south of here. Giuseppe thinks they waste their time talking to these northbounders. If they had seen something, they would have already made it known.

"What if?" Giuseppe says. . . . "What if I got up from this hole and went over to that officer and told him I know a little something about that Boy Scout? What if I told him you said you killed him and buried him under some rocks?"

"Go ahead."

The boy's nonchalant attitude surprises Giuseppe.

"I'll do it," Giuseppe says.

"You'll look like a fool. I been hitchhiking from town to town. I got all the gear but I'm what they call a Yellow-Blazer. Screw walking those mountains, I'm taking the easy way north. When I finish my thru-hike, I'm going to find me a dancer in New York City and live the good life."

"I thought you were attending Dartmouth."

The scarecrow laughs and clears his throat. "Sounded good, didn't it?"

"You're not worried about me telling Pike?"

"You won't tell him."

"I might," Giuseppe says. "I might do even worse things."

"No," Dobbs says. "You're scared. I can see it in your eyes. You're worried because you've been scamming that old man for a long time—"

"He was young when we met."

"You know what I mean. You, me, we're the same."

"We're different," Giuseppe says a little too sharply.

Giuseppe, underwear sagging at his crotch, corners Pike when he comes back from his daily co-op expedition. Pike insists that they look professional when interacting with the community and always wears designer clothes during town visits. Today he's in a dress shirt and single-pleated pants. His sunglasses, most expensive Gucci on the market, have a reflective sheen. Pike hands Giuseppe a burlap sack filled with groceries, and he follows his lover onto the porch, through the front door, and past the reading room. Two long-time customers, Janice and Heather Brougham, sit on the sofa. Janice has a PhD and studies things like snail populations in Fiji. Heather is a year older than Janice and is a doctor up in Boston. They have on matching ball caps and claim the two of them haven't stopped smiling since they voiced their vows two weeks ago up in Vermont. The smiles are a quarter inch away from turning smug and Giuseppe hates the women equally. Heather and Janice say hello, a cheesy duet, and Giuseppe nods in return. He follows his lover to the kitchen and plops the burlap sack on the counter.

"I do wish you'd get cleaned up and put some clothes on," Pike says. "Running around like a Neanderthal is bad for business."

"I'll fill that hole in and take a shower when you tell me you've changed your mind about the bathroom."

"No can do," Pike says. "Dobbs already painted it, a real pretty green."

"What?"

"Turned out nice, if you ask me."

"Fuck you, Pike."

"Giuseppe—"

"No, fuck you and that damn houseboy."

Pike lowers his voice. "I won't have you talk like that, not here, where the guests can hear you."

"Fuck, fuck, and fuck."

"What do you want?" Pike says. "Tell me what you want me to do."

"I want my share of the B&B. I want my share of the bank accounts and stock options. I want my share of everything."

"What's mine is yours. It's been that way ever since we met." Pike gets a bowl of asparagus stalks out of the refrigerator, pushes the bowl toward Giuseppe.

"Cut them into one-inch pieces," Pike says. "I'm making yellow sour curry paste tonight."

"You need salmon with that."

"I have salmon."

Giuseppe washes his hands and his arms, dries with a dishtowel hanging from one of the doors. He concentrates on the asparagus, cuts each piece in identical lengths. Pike is a perfectionist when it comes to cooking, and Giuseppe knows he'll hear about it if he doesn't do things right.

"Can you believe those two lesbos?" Giuseppe says. "They've been married for less than a month and Heather's already putting on weight."

"I hadn't noticed." Pike takes off his sunglasses and cuts pineapple into tiny cubes. The knife slices are precise and fast, almost too fast to see.

"She'll be a regular porker inside of three months." Giuseppe makes an oinking sound, and they both laugh. Pike asks if Giuseppe's seen the tamarind concentrate, and he says it's in the fridge, on the second shelf behind the olive jar.

"Thanks. Prep always goes easier when you're around."

"Glad to help, but I'm not changing my mind. I want what's coming to me and that's final."

Pike turns away in search of a wok and Giuseppe uses the temporary distraction to head to the bathroom and check out the paint job. No drip marks on the floor, but the green walls clash with the blue bath towels, blue bath mat, and blue toilet cover. Giuseppe clucks his disapproval. Whoever said green is the new blue needs a visit to the optometrist. They'll have to replace everything, no doubt a job left to Giuseppe. He goes back into the kitchen and Pike puts down his knife, crosses his arms. "We're not going to run up to Vermont just to get married."

"I'm not talking about marriage."

"It amounts to the same thing."

"Depends on how you look at it," Giuseppe says. "I could get my half and vanish."

"So you could."

"Which I would never do."

"No, I don't believe you would," Pike says.

"We've been together this long, we might as well see it out."

"Might as well."

Dobbs comes in and looks at Pike, then at Giuseppe. The boy wears matching shirt and pants—Armani—a gift for Pike that

Giuseppe purchased with his allowance two years earlier. Six inches too long, the pants bunch at the ankles.

"Talking about me?" Dobbs says.

"Leave us," Pike says, and the boy retreats to the dining room. Giuseppe and Pike stare at each other, neither looks away until Pike blinks and uncrosses his arms. "Quid pro quo. You give, you get."

"I've been giving to you more than half of my—"

"It will only take an hour of your time."

"Yeah?"

"I want a threesome," Pike says. "It's a simple equation. You fulfill my fantasy and I'll fulfill yours."

"You'd do that?" Giuseppe, facing the only lover he's ever bedded, takes a step backward.

"You're my one and only, Love. I've been telling you that for years."

The bedroom has a defunct fireplace, and on the mantel are framed photos of past vacations. Giuseppe's favorite memories come from a cruise down to the Virgin Islands, where they spent their days in ports like Frederiksted and Christiansted, sampling local dishes. Pike preferred conch over white rice, although, in typical Pike fashion, he complained the seasoning wasn't balanced. Giuseppe favored red snapper basted in garlic butter and washed everything down with rum. He remembers thinking rum was so cheap that if they lived in the islands he'd wake up every morning with a hangover. At night he left his small berth and walked up two decks to Pike's suite, where he waited until the hall was clear before entering. Sex was brief but spectacular and afterward they cuddled on silk sheets and ate caviar and crackers.

Giuseppe now grasps a photo and brings it close to his eyes, moves it away and Pike's face comes into focus. He wears a beige T-shirt and white shorts, and his hair is tangled from the wind. Behind him, a rippled inlet reflects the sun. Giuseppe puts the photo back and walks over to the window. They were so young back then, each concealing his sexuality, a secret that wrapped around them like an invisible cocoon. Times have changed, and now the whole world seems different. They live in a town full of *tolerant* people. Pike and Giuseppe go where they want, when they want, and no one cares. Giuseppe misses the covert glance, the thrill of the secret rendezvous. When their relationship was new, Pike didn't need another to feel complete, certainly not some acne-faced hustler trying to make a buck.

Giuseppe parts the curtains, looks down at three tents in a rainbow triangle. Never Lost, Tazmanian Devil, and Red Bear have stayed overnight. His instinct tells him Never Lost and Tazmanian Devil are a couple, even though they don't act like it in public. Red Bear is an Indian, and he has the shiniest black hair Giuseppe has ever seen. He'd like to get to know them better, especially Tazmanian Devil, who has this hunk of a jaw and curly brown hair, but hikers at the B&B are an ever-changing group, here today, gone tomorrow, and making friends with someone who will soon leave is a waste of time. Some days he wants to put on a backpack and follow them down the trail. North, south, the direction doesn't matter, so long as it's anywhere but here.

Dobbs and Pike walk into the bedroom and nausea comes over Giuseppe, a light-headedness that threatens to topple him to the floor. Dobbs takes off his clothes and hops in bed. He has a tattoo of a snake on his chest; venom drips from pink fangs.

"Come over here," the boy says. "Let me make a man out of you."

Giuseppe kisses his lover roughly on the lips. Pike returns the kiss and in a scramble of creaky arms and legs, they join the boy. For the next hour, Giuseppe exists in a timeless fog, moans and whispered words too dispersed to comprehend. He dreams of the bottom line, thinks of the papers he will sign.

In the utility shed, Dobbs at his side, Giuseppe pours gas from a red can into the John Deere. The shed smells like grease and gas and dusty corners and is the only room on the property Pike never visits. Auto parts, left over from the previous owner, sit on yellowed newspapers with dates as far back as the 1960s. Jars and tin cans on the workbench hold random assortments of nails, screws, nuts and bolts, fasteners, assorted extension cords, and electrical sockets. The effect, so many things in so many places, reminds Giuseppe of controlled chaos, and he supposes the shed is fitting locale for the conversation he's been having with the boy.

"You should have asked for my ID before we hit the sack," Dobbs says. He tilts a half-empty bottle of Chablis from the collection in the cellar, swallows, and wipes his mouth on his sleeve. "Hell, I'm not but fourteen."

"What do you mean you're 'not but fourteen'?" Giuseppe asks. He entwines his fingers in the boy's hair, yanks his head upwards. His breath, so close to Giuseppe's face, smells like fermented bubble gum. Dobbs's eyes are glassy, open but seeing nothing.

"Let me go."

"What do you mean you're 'not but fourteen'?"

"Fuck damn," Dobbs says. "Be fifteen March."

"You little shit." Giuseppe turns the boy loose and sets down the gas can.

"I ain't nobody's fool. You homos fucked me in the ass and came in my mouth and made me do things no child should bear. That's what I'll tell the police next time they come to visit. I'll tell them you raped me in the bedroom. I'll describe both your dicks and that little mole on your balls and you'll both get twenty years."

Cold creeps into Giuseppe's bones. He spent the morning waiting for Pike to come back from the bank, hoping his lover, no, that's not right, *knowing* his lover will honor his word. Pike has money, and plenty of it, which means Giuseppe will soon be rich. He can afford to buy off the boy.

"I'll give you a hundred dollars," Giuseppe says. "You go away and never come back."

"Shit."

"Pike fired you first thing this morning."

The boy does a strange hopping dance, a wobbly skeleton in designer clothes. "He needs someone to take care of the house."

"That's my job."

"*Pow*," the boy says, and points his finger at Giuseppe's chest. "*Pow! Pow! Pow!* Was your job, your wrinkled ass is packing up and leaving."

"I'll give you fifty thousand."

The boy stumbles and grabs the workbench, knocks a jar to the floor. Shattered glass and screws scatter across concrete. He rights himself, brushes off his clothes. "Me and Pike will get married and I'll fuck him to death. I will fuck your sugar daddy so hard he'll be dead inside a year."

"He's got a million in the garden, in a safe buried under the broccoli. You leave us alone and it's yours."

"A million?" The boy's eyes clear, only for a moment, and the glaze returns.

"Cash, some jewelry—"

"I always wanted one of them gold necklaces like a music video pimp." He takes another swallow. "That's what I'm talking about."

"He has gold necklaces and rings and a diamond bracelet so shiny it'll make your eyes hurt."

"Bullshit."

"Suit yourself."

Giuseppe picks up a shovel and walks out of the shade into the sun. He blinks blindness from his eyes, steps over the carrot row, and walks around the fast-growing zucchini. A ladybug lands on his hand and he flicks the bug away and walks deeper into the garden, pauses when he comes to the hole. It seems so long ago he lay at the bottom staring up at the sky. Dobbs stands ten feet away, wine bottle at his feet. He looks lost, a tourist at an intersection and no map in sight.

"I think I drank too fast." A stain starts at the bottom of the boy's zipper, spreads outward. "I think I should have slowed down."

"Hey," Giuseppe says, "ever see a praying mantis?"

"A what?"

"It's a bug that eats other bugs, rips their guts out and everything."

The boy looks interested. "It rips out their guts?"

"They sort of remind me of you," Giuseppe says. "They sneak up on you, then move in for the kill."

The boy thrashes through the corn and stops short of the hole. "I can't see him."

"He's about a foot from the ground. See, he's on the stem, stalking that caterpillar."

The boy sags to his knees, clutches dirt in both hands. The praying mantis, a twig with matchstick legs and bulbous eyes, closes in on its prey. Giuseppe always feels sorry when he sees a bug about to die, but he never interferes with nature. In the garden, the strong survive.

"Look," the boy says. "That's me and you."

"So it is."

"You're the caterpillar," the boy says. "You sucked yourself right in with Pike and now you're fat and happy and about to die."

"You got me to a tee, Dobbs, you nailed me to the wall." Giuseppe studies the house, looks for open curtains, a patron on the porch, glances at the campsites and sees only trees and tents. He grips the shovel handle, nails digging into the wood, and raises the blade. Giuseppe stares at the boy's neck, at the spine at the base of the skull, imagines the swift arc, the downward thrust, the spray of blood and the crunch of metal against bone. It would be so easy, one *thwack*, then fill in the hole and forget about him. A coolness comes over Giuseppe, a chilliness that spreads through his extremities. He shivers and raises the blade high. Lowers it when he spots movement out of the corner of his eye. It's Tazmanian Devil, who crawls out of his tent and drapes a sleeping bag over a picnic table. Giuseppe lowers the shovel and kicks Dobbs into the hole.

"You don't know how lucky you are," Giuseppe says.

"Oh," the boy says, and falls on his back.

Giuseppe clambers down and presses the shovel point against the quivering throat. The boy squirms and mouths words that don't come.

"What?" Giuseppe says. "What did you say?"

"I was fucking with you." The boy turns his head and vomits into the dirt. "I'm a month over eighteen. Are you crazy or what?"

Giuseppe grabs the boy's head, drives it into the earth. The chilliness is still there and Giuseppe is so cold he is shaking.

"Eighteen or fourteen," he says. "I don't give a shit. You hurt Pike and bad things will happen. Do you understand me? Something very bad will happen."

Candles flicker on the dining room table, turn the champagne glasses into shimmering mirages. Pike's cologne drifts through the air. The aroma is rich and sweet and reminds Giuseppe of summer walks in meadows thick with flowers. Pike wears his robe, but Giuseppe chose something more formal for the occasion: shirt and tie, black pants, and a pair of brown loafers one size too small. He wears the toe squeezers for a reason. They are his pinch on the arm, the self-invoked pain that reminds him this is really happening. Pike removes papers from a briefcase, and he and Giuseppe lean forward.

"This one," Pike says, and hands Giuseppe a gold pen, "is a mutual-fund account I opened around the time I was offered senior partner. Remember the party we had afterward? You and me drinking all those martinis? I had such a hangover the next day."

Giuseppe starts the ballpoint rolling with a downward curve, signs first and last name, ends with a triumphant swoop. The fund is worth 1.2 million. Pike hands over another paper and Giuseppe signs again, half interest in an office building in Philadelphia, an investment Pike says is paid off and worth 3.5 million last time he had it appraised, which was back in the late nineties so it's worth a lot more now.

"I knew you had money," Giuseppe says, "but I really had no idea."

"*We* had money."

"I knew *we* had money but this is crazy."

"You were going to get it all, sooner or later," Pike says. "You are the sole beneficiary in my will."

"I don't even have a will." Giuseppe loosens his tie and works his toes, eases the pain shooting through his feet.

"We'll need to draw one up for you. Or maybe you'll want to go to another attorney and have it done. That's a very private occasion."

"You can do it, Pike. It's not like I have anything to hide."

Giuseppe signs his name on nineteen more pieces of paper—various stocks, insurance funds, and savings accounts—drops the pen to the table and leans back in his chair.

"Listen," Pike says, "feel free to paint the bathroom back the way it was. I guess you really don't like chartreuse."

"I'll get used to it."

"Dobbs did a nice job."

"Yes, he did," Giuseppe says.

"Do you know what he said to me after I fired him?"

"That boy was liable to say anything."

Pike sips champagne and stacks papers into a neat pile. "He tried to extort money, said he was only fourteen years old. Said by the time he was done with us he'd own the B&B."

"Well, he's gone now." Giuseppe rolls the pen across the table, one way, then the other.

"You took care of the problem?"

"Let's just say he decided to hike north."

Pike pours champagne, a swirl of silver bubbles. "He reminded me of you, you know? When you were young."

"Yeah?"

"Take away the acne, dye his hair black, and you could have been twins."

One of the candles goes out, and Giuseppe holds a match to the wick. It won't relight and he gives up. "I was a hustler."

"Yes, you were."

"I hustled you into giving me a place to stay."

"Yes, you did," Pike says.

Giuseppe closes his eyes and tilts his head back. "Have any regrets? Anything you wish you could take back?"

"About us?"

"Anything, anything at all."

Pike waits awhile before answering. "None I'm aware of. You?"

Giuseppe takes off his loafers and studies Pike's face, wonders how he would have reacted if roles had been reversed in the garden. Would Pike kill for his lover? A melancholy comes over Giuseppe, a roaring sound across a barren land. He braces against the relentless wind, faces the loneliness of his world.

9

SIMONE AND I have hiked into Vermont, our twelfth state, and today a smattering of rain blankets the trees. The clouds open and close, send random shafts of sunlight through the leaves, a mottled landscape of greens and browns that lighten and darken the forest floor. A clearing in front of us opens to a large pond and we stop and sit on a log, drink from our water bottles, and eat a snack. A rainbow trout flashes against the surface, a fusion of red and silver, and the swirl it leaves behind ripples across the waves. Frogs peep in the weeds near the shoreline, a chorus that seems to grow louder the wetter it gets. Across the pond, deer ghost in and out of the trees, their brown backs turning gray in the shadows.

"Roxie and I go way back," I say. "There's nothing between me and her like you're thinking."

True to the words Simone spoke back at Pen Mar Park, she only fucks me when we are on the trail. In town she gets a motel room and so do I. In town she acts like I'm a stranger. She plays a control game, and I willingly follow along. Part-time pussy is better than none at all.

I touch her elbow, and she jerks her arm away. My hand drops to the log, to the soggy moss and rotted bark. In my other life, I would have washed off my gritty palm. In the mountains, life is different. There are no sinks, no paper towels, and now, judging the ferocity in Simone's gaze, no girlfriend.

"Taz," she says. "You don't need my permission to go back to your cokehead lover."

"She's only coming for a visit, twenty-four hours and she'll be gone."

"You are such a loser."

Simone walks down the trail and doesn't look back. I shouldn't have told her about Roxie and our drug problems, but getting it out in the open is my way of moving on. When I lived in Atlanta, I did things no human should do. But I'm no longer *that* guy. I think that's what pisses Simone off the most. I'm *proof* her DNA theory is flawed.

I wait for an hour, then walk north. She has the tent in her backpack. I'll need to find Richard or a shelter if I want to sleep dry tonight.

That evening, I walk up on my friend in front of a campfire. He gave up his loincloth when the mosquitoes got bad and now wears long pants and a long-sleeve shirt. Next to him, strips of meat lay on a flat rock. He sharpens a stick, skewers a strip, swings the stick toward the flame.

"Blacksnake," he says. "Cook your own."

Richard showed me pictures of his mother and father on the ranch in Montana, and yes, they are blond haired, blue eyed, and look like they flew in from Denmark, but I don't buy his theory an Indian gene hides for generations in his family, then emerges and produces a Blackfoot carbon copy. His mother slept with someone on the reservation and that's how Richard got his high forehead and ink-black hair. In his real life Richard is a tire salesman. He can name every brand, every size, wholesale and retail costs.

"I thought the snake was your spirit guide," I say. "Or was it the bear? I can never remember that shit."

"It might be the eagle."

I take off my pack and sit on the ground. My ass has been in the rain all day long, so it's not like it can get any wetter. Least, for the moment, the sky has cleared.

"You can't change your spirit guide," I say. "That's like one day saying you're Catholic and the next you're Baptist."

"I was hungry."

"You're out of food?" I ask.

"I was hungry for something that isn't in my pack."

Richard swings the stick away from the flame and blows on the meat. He is the only hiker I know who can start a fire in a soaked forest. He's a natural. I boil water and cook a dish I've worked on for the last couple of weeks, a seasoned rice that I mix with chocolate oatmeal. I sprinkle in two drops of Louisiana hot sauce.

"I'm using less spices these days. Brings out the chocolate flavor," I say.

He eats his snake and I eat my rice and oatmeal. The evening turns to darkness, and I throw a log on the fire, watch flames curl around the bark, listen to my white Indian friend make guzzling noises when he swallows. I tell him about arguing with Simone and proclaim her a bitch through and through.

"I've never even seen her take a break on a cliff," I say. "What kind of hiker is scared of heights?"

"Maybe she thinks you'll push her off."

It's a bad joke, brings up the memory of the dead guy Richard and I burned at the base of the cliff down in Georgia. I shove the memory back into its hiding place. There are some things I'd rather not think about. Richard gets out his bottle and offers me a drink. I sip and hand it back. He laughs, a crazy fucking sound, and drinks a quarter of the bottle in one long swallow.

"I wish I had your self-control," he says. "I wish I could sip instead of guzzle."

He leaps to his feet and hovers over the flames, extends his arms, and the smell of singed hair mixes with wood smoke.

"The white man," he says, "stole this land. They raped and murdered and took what wasn't theirs. They killed with guns and cannon and knives and chicken pox."

"Knives and chicken pox," I say. "Guns and cannon."

He sheds his clothes, and firelight turns his skin into a red-hued shadow. "My people were like the trees and the air. We were *everywhere*. Then the white man came and took it from us. I have a white mother, true. And I have a white father, that also is true. But my blood is red and in my chest beats the heart of a warrior."

"Will you shut up," I say. "You're giving me a headache with all this Indian shit."

Richard swings his arms in time with his feet and throws back his head. He stomps clockwise around the fire, pauses, and drinks more whiskey. He staggers and I jump up and grab his shoulder, sit him with his back against a tree. I rummage through his pack and get out his tent, pitch it in the firelight, then unroll his sleeping bag. I haul him upright and guide him inside. He sprawls diagonally. I don't have the heart to push him aside, which means there is no room for me, so I sit next to the fire. Above, stars speckle the sky, winks of light on a black background, and I sit for a long time without moving. Clouds move back in, bring a quick shower, and I face the rain without blinking an eye. The clouds leave and the stars return, the fire now a smoldering memory. I think of my father and how he enjoyed the outdoors from time to time. He took me places, like to see horses in the desert, but back then I was an outsider in the wild. Now things are different. I've been on the trail for so long I feel it coursing through my veins. The AT has become my lifeblood, my sustenance, and sitting in the rain in the middle of the forest feels like the most natural thing in the world.

A breeze whispers out of the darkness, a coolness over my skin, and I kneel and blow across the coals until they flame upward. From a nearby tree, I break off a dead branch, snap it into pieces, drop them into the pit. The breeze switches direction, and flames bend toward my legs. I step away from the heat and the smoke, pat my pockets for a snack.

A twig snaps and I swivel to peer into blackness, see Simone's face reflecting the firelight. I lunge into the forest, hear crashing in the brush. I call out her name and no one answers.

Richard thinks the weather god is a she. Mine swings both ways. On good days, she's a she. On bad days, he's a he. Today, as we ascend Killington Peak, a mountain that tops out at 4,235 feet, the weather god is a soggy bastard. Water runs down the trail in miniature creeks, veers into eroded ditches that V into ferned-over slopes, only to start anew like an eternal spring put on this earth to annoy hikers. My feet have been wet for three days. My shirt and pants cling to my skin in sodden clumps. The storm comes in waves, bands of a hurricane that angled away from land but is determined to leave a mark. Clouds whip past in long shreds that shadow the forest for minutes at a time.

Simone's right foot turns outward more than her left. Sometimes her footprints are close together and sometimes they are stretched out, like she hears me coming and jogs to put distance between us. I've done Downward Facing Dog ten times a day since she showed it to me, and my foot pain has disappeared. If I want to catch her, I can. I speed up, strides that squish into the mud.

An hour later I see her on a switchback. She has an odd walking style, a semi-crouch like she creeps up on something, arms that cock at her elbows and swing out of rhythm with her legs.

The trees, the steel-colored boulders, the muddy footpath, congeal into a watery mosaic that absorbs edges and stretches shapes into long curves. I blink away the moisture, watch the world refit itself. She has a determined stride, but I walk up behind her soon enough.

"Hey," I say.

She looks over her shoulder.

"You might have told me it wasn't over between you and Roxie."

Simone starts walking faster but she can't out-walk me and eventually realizes the futility and slows down. Which is a good thing because we will soon be above treeline, close to the top of this mountain, and no sane hiker will chance electrocution to avoid an uncomfortable conversation. I walk toward her, and she walks up the trail. I stop and she stops. We repeat this several times, then I grin like the game has been fun, tell her we should wait out the storm, watch her walk up the trail. Expecting her to come back, I wait a few minutes. When she doesn't, I follow her to where the trail exits the trees and winds around the side of a rocky summit. I move quickly, trying to limit exposure, see her leave the AT and scramble up a blue blaze trail that leads to the peak.

She reaches the top, looks down at me, and seems to be saying something. Wind and rain gouge at her words, and all I hear is the storm across the Appalachians. Above her the clouds are nasty colors of gray and black, bruises that slide over the peak and rush onward. She raises her arms and extends her middle fingers. Light bridges heaven and earth, an explosion to her left, and a sizzling spiderweb scuttles toward her. The air turns green, like I'm looking through night-vision goggles. Another bolt, and she disappears in the flash like she disintegrated, only that isn't possible and before I know it I'm running up the slope. The granite is slick and I lose my footing. I slide down, regain my balance, scramble upward until I arrive at where she lies on the rocks. Her eyes roll back in their sockets, and I shake her until she focuses. I help her to her feet, down the blue blaze trail, back to the AT, where I press my palm against her back and guide her into the relative safety of the trees. I tell her if she had been standing twenty feet to the right, that bolt would have fried her top to bottom. She regains her bearings a little at a time, and a quarter-mile down the ridge says something I will never forget.

"My mouth tastes like pennies."

Then she says something else.

"I wish I was dead."

I didn't think our breakup was *that* big of a deal.

*   *   *

In the motel parking lot in Norwich, a town a few miles from the New Hampshire border, a used Toyota pulls up and the driver steps into the twilight. I have been on the trail for over four months and in that time Roxie's cheeks have thickened. Her skinny, haunted look is gone. Instead of T-shirt and jeans, she has on a beige dress and high heels that click the asphalt. I've known her for years and never heard her click when she walked. I wasn't sure what to expect, know it wasn't a Toyota and high heels.

We walk inside, out of the shadows, into the light of my room. If Roxie notices the trail smells, she doesn't say anything. Least I'm clean. Took four showers and washed clothes, applied deodorant under my armpits.

"So," Roxie says. "Here I am."

"You look good."

"So do you."

We sit across from each other, a round table between us, make several attempts at small talk like ex-lovers do when they try to find their way back to each other. Memories from our past are impossible to sort out, and our conversation is a series of dead ends. We didn't get much sleep when we were together, that I remember. She has a distracted look, like she can't remember why she's here.

"If we get back together, you got to promise me some things," she says. "You got to make some fucking changes."

Roxie ticks off a list, which starts with no drugs and alcohol and ends with no staying out all night. She's moved into an apartment and works for a travel agency in northern Atlanta. Right now she only takes phone calls, but she has a chance to make something of herself and doesn't want to screw it up.

"I don't even think about it anymore," I say.

We talk about *it*, never once saying *coke* out loud. She's off *it* for good. Thinks *it* came close to killing her but now she sees the light. I tell her I haven't even thought of *it* since I started walking the mountains, add that *it* is in the past for me.

"My thru-hike is going well," I say. "I'm a purist, which means I'm walking every foot of the trail and not taking shortcuts."

She looks around the room, like she sees my gear for the first time, and a narrowness invades the flesh between her eyes. My tent hangs from the bathroom door, and food bags are strewn across the carpet. My sleeping bag blankets the air conditioner in the window. I'm like every other hiker who walks out of a wet forest, I dry my gear when I get to town. This is not a bad thing. I open my data book and point out the mileage, tell her about the springs and the shelters, and how it took me a long time to walk into hiking shape.

"New Hampshire and Maine," I say. "Two states left to go."

Roxie drags a brush through her hair. A ripping sound. Like there are tangles she will never get out. She makes a flicking motion, as though she clears the air before starting a new conversation. "I want you to pack up and come back to Atlanta. If it goes well, you can move in with me. But not right away. . . . We have to see first."

I touch her cheek, want to ignite something inside me. My hand lingers for a long time. She stares at her purse like she wants to pick it up and leave. I should have known she would ask me to choose between my life and hers. The phone rings and I pick up the receiver.

"Hello?" I say.

The hiss of a bad connection, someone breathing.

"I cut my wrist with a razor but you needn't worry," Simone says. "It didn't go deep enough."

Drama queen comes to mind, then an image of a man tied between horses straining in opposite directions. I have a choice, get off the trail and try to make a life with Roxie, or continue hiking into an unknown that may or may not contain Simone. I study Roxie, take in the dress and the searching green eyes, come to a decision I hope I don't regret.

"Meet me in the parking lot," I say into the phone.

I tell Roxie I'll be back, slip outside. The town is spread out and has a white glow that washes out the stars. Cars and trucks drive down the highway, and the smells of oil, gasoline, and a catalytic converter tinge the breeze, scents that didn't bother me pre-trail but now nauseate me. Simone steps out of a room five doors down and heads toward the street.

"Hey," I say.

She does not turn around. I jog up to her, and, in the glare of oncoming headlights, spot the nick on her wrist. The cut is an inch long, over the vein, and barely deep enough to break skin. I follow her into town, where we parallel show windows so glassy and dark they remind me of black ice.

A siren sounds, my old instincts kick in, and I duck into an alley that smells like fish. Simone merges with the shadows. The squad car drives past, blue lights licking at the buildings, then the night returns. Soon as my eyes adjust, I skirt a box-filled Dumpster and she follows me through the litter. We walk past cats squalling on a stoop, past mattresses propped up against buildings. We kick cans across the asphalt. Simone communicates in monosyllables.

Yes, she thinks I'm an asshole. No, she's not afraid to walk in alleys. Yes, she likes to walk at night. We leave the business district, cross a street, and drift past fenced-in backyards. Dogs bark and inside the houses the glow of late-night television flickers across the curtains.

Houses thin out and soon we walk past the city-limit sign and arrive in the country. Here, there is no light to fade out the stars, and they flicker against the blackness like fiery sequins, millions of them, as though every star mankind has ever seen has decided to show itself at this very moment. Simone has a fresh-washed smell, a fruity scent that makes me hungry in more ways than one.

"I love you," I say.

Simone mimics my words. I don't love her and she knows it and that's the problem. She doesn't need to hear that lie.

We come to a house, a single story set off the road, in a field partially lit by a rectangle of light spilling out of a window. A woman, framed by open drapes, reads on a sofa in a living room. I cut through the grass, to the shadows next to a rusted swing set, motion to Simone. She arrives in that familiar crouch, and we face the window.

The woman, wearing a housecoat, sits in a recliner. Her legs curl under her hips, and toes peek out from beneath yellow folds. She holds a book that has a picture of a bare-chested man on the cover, and her face has a glow, an intensity, like she's inside what she's reading. I come up with an idea, something crazy that I hope closes the distance between Simone and me.

"Let's break in and steal something."

"I want no part of this." Simone backs away.

The moon is over the trees, and there's enough light to see her outline on the road, not enough to make out her features. I creep to the window and straighten enough to see inside. Pictures of Venice, the Eiffel Tower, and island beaches—in silver picture frames—hang on the walls. The woman has big bones, a girl who grew up on the farm and carried milk pails every morning. Her hair is blond and her skin is pale, her fingernails are long and buffed at the end. She is the salt of the earth. The woman needs a name, and I decide on Sybil. My Sybil is a romantic. She likes faraway places, vacations best shared with a lover. I was wrong about the book. There's also a woman on the cover. She's kneeling and looking up at the man, has a rapturous expression. *Rapturous*. I like that word.

Simone hisses, a drawn out, angry *pssst*. I ignore her and she hisses again. A thump, a dribble across the grass.

Simone is throwing rocks.

"Come over here," she says.

Another rock, then another and another. They fall short, a product of piddly tosses from someone who apparently has never played baseball, and I conclude she doesn't have much of an arm. I cup my hands and whisper in her direction.

"You throw like a girl."

The next rock lands closer and I realize she does have an arm and not only that, she also has aim. She bends over the ditch at the side of the road, digs around, straightens, and hurls another rock my way. This one lands at my feet. I pick it up and throw it back, aim it over her head, into the trees on the other side of the road. Another rock lands at my feet.

"I don't know what you're trying to prove," she says.

I raise my fists above the sill, enough so I'm sure she can see them, extend my middle fingers. Mimicking her posture the day she was almost struck by lightning is funny, and I hold back a laugh. The next rock comes out of the darkness into the light. Flat trajectory, like the rock has energy behind it. I notice this because I know what's going to happen and in that knowledge comes a slowing down that enables me to see minute detail. The rock, round and dull gray, tumbles like an asteroid on a collision course. There is no taking this rock back. It's thrown, hurled really, approximately seven feet off the ground, and soon will reach its destination. I can only watch the rock sail over my head, can only listen to the rock impact glass, a million cracks spreading in all directions. I duck and run from the shrillness within. I run down the road, and Simone runs with me.

We hear the squad car before we see it, duck behind trees, veer back on the road as the car passes. Simone laughs so hard she doubles over.

"I can't believe I did that," she says.

She presses against me like she wants to fuck right there in the weeds, and I tell her we need to put distance between us and the house. We run into town, stretched-out strides, arms pumping in time with the asphalt thuds. We slow to a trot and make our way through the alley, past the cats and rotting mattresses, to the motel parking lot.

Roxie's car is gone, and I'm relieved she didn't need a break-up conversation. Richard has a room at the far end of the motel, and his light is on. The door is open. I knock, he doesn't answer, so we walk in, step over his gear, peek into the bathroom expecting to find him passed out in the tub. Empty. A half-full bottle on the table, alongside his data book. A groan from under the bed, Simone looks, says he's passed out.

She gets her pack from her room, and we go inside mine. I

read a note from Roxie, wad up the paper into a tiny ball, toss it in the wastebasket. Her coming up was a bad idea all around. It's over between us, her exact words, and I tell Simone I have closure. Closure. That's like walking through a door that doesn't open from the other side, which is okay with me as far as Roxie is concerned. We only had *it* between us. Take *it* away and there is no us.

I cradle Simone's wrist, bring the cut to my lips. I explore the edges with my tongue, suck at the wound, taste the salty skin.

10

LEONA, IN THE waiting room, holds her purse on her lap while she waits for word about Emanuel. Across from her, a young man and a young woman sit one chair apart and between them, in the middle chair, kneels a child who scratches her patchy scalp. The young man has calloused hands and brown skin. The couple hovers over their offspring like their physical closeness will protect her from evil.

Leona is in need of shelter and wishes her parents were alive to offer encouraging words, but she is old and her parents are dead. If Parker was here, her youngest, he would tell a joke and regale her with a comical scene from his travels. Heather, her oldest, is in the hospital, in another wing, where she delivers Boston babies at the rate of several a day. She has promised to look in before Leona and Emanuel head back to New Hampshire.

"Nice weather we're having today," Leona says.

The man and woman glance up, turn their attention back to their child. Leona looks down at her own hands and watches her fingers entwine and separate, a synchronized movement of wrinkled skin and sweaty palms. One part of her wants to escape the hospital unscathed and another part wants a diagnosis that explains Emanuel's erratic behavior.

She accommodated his desire that they experiment with multiple sex partners, had separated body and soul to endure his perversions, but yesterday's experience in the grocery store had convinced her that she needed to seek help. They were in the dairy aisle—trying to recall whether they preferred two percent or low fat—when he pointed at an overweight woman who pushed a cart filled with potato chip bags and donut boxes. The smell of salami drifted from the nearby deli.

"Look at that cow," Emanuel said. "If those titties get any bigger, they'll have to hook her up to a milking machine."

The woman waddled away, Emanuel's voice loud behind her. Leona was appalled and when she and her husband returned home, she called Heather, who promptly scheduled an emergency appointment with a neurologist.

Footsteps now come down the hallway, and Leona peers around the corner. She wears a print dress, and her flowery hat is pinned to her hair so tightly the fabric feels like part of her cranium. She watches a nurse walk past, full of purpose, white hose a whisper with each step.

Leona's right leg is asleep from sitting, so she gets up and stands in front of her chair. Anyone looking at her will think she suffers from indecision, unable to make up her mind to sit or stand, but there is no one in the room except the young man and the young woman and the little girl, and they haven't even asked her name.

Leona looks down at the child. The girl, who has a turned-down mouth, is made uglier by whatever illness afflicts her body. Leona chastises herself for the thought, gets a gumdrop out of her purse, holds out her hand. When her offering goes unnoticed, she pops the candy in her mouth and sucks the lemony flavor. She thinks lemon is her favorite, although she can't remember for sure. It might be cherry. The child squalls, and Leona sits down. The young woman holds the girl and stares straight ahead, while the brown-skinned man glances at Leona and apologizes.

"For what?" Leona says.

Late summer, and the New Hampshire mountains, framed by the picture window in the living room, thrust against the sky. Leona, who once sought inspiration from this view, hardly notices as she helps Emanuel into his recliner. Her husband wears a robe and a diaper, has developed a twitch in his right eye and right hand. She runs her fingers through his yellow hair. Chemo would have been pointless, the tumor so large and entwined in Emanuel's brain the neurologist said he only had a month to live. If the prediction is correct, her husband will pass away in nine days. She sniffs the air, at the staleness that invades the house. The smell might be from the garbage under the sink. She makes a mental note to empty the container, and seconds later the reminder to remember evaporates from her brain.

She pinches Emanuel's arm, hard enough to break skin, and blood seeps out, forming two half moons. She pinches him again, studies the glaze over his eyes.

"Goddamn it to hell," she says.

There are days when she wishes he would get it over with so she could put him in their family plot in Evergreen Cemetery.

Parker, in the garage, sings a loud song about a one-eyed

woman who loved a toe-less dwarf. Leona smiles because she knows he sings to perk up her spirits. He has moved home to care for his father until the end. Heather comes up when she can.

Leona wipes spittle off Emanuel's mouth, brings her face close to the window, wishes she could remember where she put the binoculars. This is the season when the northbounders, up from Georgia, traverse the mountain. She has watched them in years past. Their packs come in all colors, and sometimes they walk in twos and threes. Mostly they are alone.

"Mom," Parker says from the hallway, "I do wish you'd get out of the house today."

Parker has his father's hair, his father's mouth. She looks at Parker and sees Emanuel, she looks at Emanuel and sees shriveled skin and a rotted brain. Emanuel squirms and slides toward the floor, and she drags him upright. His robe falls open and she covers him up and reties the sash. Her husband would remain unshaven if it weren't for her scraping a razor against his cheek each morning. She straps his watch on his wrist, even though he can no longer tell time. On some days, knowing he occasionally read before the illness, she places a novel in his lap. Her children think she wastes her energy. Leona does these things anyway. To stop feels like giving up and she does not have a give-up bone in her body.

Her son flings his arms around her, and she feels small in his hug. She loves him when he does this, when he squeezes hard with no inclination to let go. She wants to cry but this is not a time for weakness. He steps away and presses the car keys into her hands.

"Get the hell out of here, Mom."

"Are you sure?" she says.

Her far-wandering son has returned from his travels. She wishes he was here under different circumstances.

"Go!" he says.

On the cliff, Leona hands a cookie to a hiker who eats it in two gulps. The hiker has a trail name, which she forgets soon as she hears it. He has reddish skin, fine black hair, cheekbones flat as plates, and he wishes her well as he hikes up the trail. She returns to the edge, close enough so she can see down the rock wall into the thick forest. The creek that winds through the pasture at the bottom sparkles like silver minnows school on its surface. She and Emanuel fished in that creek when they were young. They caught rainbow trout and grilled them over an open fire. They made love in that pasture, water purling over the rocks, under moonlight so bright their bodies glowed.

Leona wipes her eyes and blinks to clear her vision. She thinks she might confuse this pasture with another, brushes that thought away. They made love in a pasture when they were young, that she knows with certainty.

Footsteps behind her, light and quick, and because she does not want to explain her tears, she does not turn and say hello. She hopes whoever it is will put her lack of acknowledgment to a deaf ear and leave her be. The breeze quickens, a cooling across her skin, and she tilts her face upwards. Clouds drift against an off-white sky. When she was young, she saw animals in the clouds and now she just sees clouds. Whoever is behind her has stopped, or maybe has moved on and she has forgotten. She wishes she had dominion over her memories. If she could choose, she would forget about old Emanuel and remember him in his twenties. So young, a promise of their shared future in his gaze.

The thrust—the palm that drives into her back, the flattening of her blouse between her shoulder blades, the buckle of her knees and the flail of her arms—happens so fast that for a fraction of a second she thinks she toppled on her own, a calamity she could have avoided if she had been more careful. But then the wind blows against her face and she rushes down along that long gray wall and knows someone from above pushed her.

She twists her neck but cannot see from this angle, and she turns back toward the earth below. She's heard that people relive their lives at the moment before death, that time slows until it hardly moves. She wishes to emerge from this free fall reborn, bursting inside with a vision of all that came before. Mostly she wants to feel the touch of her yellow-haired lover, the smoothness of his skin, the tautness of his back while his body moves over hers.

She closes her eyes and her life unreels through her mind, a series of scenes that come through so fast they are a shattered collage that won't congeal into a sensible pattern. She wills them to slow and a scene early in her life crystallizes, one of a young girl in pigtails, a child who picks a handful of daisies and runs through the yard. It is summer, air balmy against her skin, and she wears hiking boots that flop with each stride. They are her father's boots, much too large, but then she is an oddball child and given to such irregularities.

The little girl disappears and two scenes merge together. Leona shakes her head, tries to see one scene at a time, but Heather and Parker are delivered almost simultaneously. They have big heads and big ears and no hair. Emanuel peeks through a crack in the door and frowns each time, like he cannot believe he fathered something so ugly. But then he is beside her, assuring her that all the fingers and toes are there, and that Heather looks just like her mother, cute as a button, and that Parker already looks like a little linebacker.

The scenes switch off and Leona opens her eyes, stretches her arms to the rock wall, hopes to catch hold of a nook, a cranny, something to disrupt her fall. Her arm cracks against the granite and the bone separates in her shoulder. No pain, only a curiousness over the flopping appendage.

She hears the rattle of Emanuel's old truck, a scene from when she was in her twenties. He has the headlights off and navigates a forest road only using the moon. Her yellow-haired lover has a wandering hand on nights like these, and her breaths come in bursts, small and quick, a hotness that turns to liquid in her veins. She lives for these drives, for that touch, for the merging of her body and his.

Halfway down now, or perhaps three-quarters. The wind blurs her eyes and she braces herself for the impact. She hopes whoever is up there is watching; she does not want to die alone. But then, what does it really matter? Alone or with someone, death cannot be shared. She feels the gravity push against her pelvis, she feels her hands clutch the emptiness of air. And then her body hits the trees, breaking through branches, snaps loud as the explosions in Emanuel's war tape. She thinks of the cookies in the Baggie in her pocket and does not know why. Then there is a graying, a light that darkens until she sees no more.

11

RICHARD AND I drop our packs and sit in ferns that grow at the edge of a pond. He points out a jack in the pulpit, says they are one of his favorite flowers. The Maine hardwood forest is changing color, and red and yellow leaves adorn the branches, a pleasant enough scene, but one that also reminds me that fall, and sometimes snow, comes early this far north. We have been discussing the Kennebec River crossing, where an upstream dam opens its gates and sends millions of gallons toward the Atlantic Ocean, a controlled flood that years back killed a fording hiker. Now the Appalachian Trail Committee and the local hiking club pay an employee to ferry hikers during the season.

"I walked all the way from Georgia," Richard says, "and I refuse to make forward progress with anything but my feet."

"Simone wants us to take the canoe across."

"Whipped as you are that must be some damn fine pussy." Richard plans an early crossing and hopes the water level doesn't rise. Claims he's one Indian who can't swim for shit. He gets out a bottle—he's gone back to Scotch—doesn't offer me any. I unwrap a candy bar and eat it in two bites. I swapped my affinity for coke for hiking and chocolate. Definite upgrade.

In the trees to the south, Simone appears in her familiar crouch, walks up, and drops her pack next to mine. She strips off her sports bra and shorts and wades into the pond. I strip and wade in beside her. The water is cool. The bottom is sandy between my toes. Richard packs his bottle away and walks up the trail without saying a word. He thinks I chose Simone over him.

She wraps her arms around me and I tread into deeper water. She floats, legs encircling my body. I like the weightlessness. The feel of her skin next to mine. We drift to the center of the pond, watch falling leaves flit like erratic butterflies through the air. Water bugs skate over the ripples. Simone and I are in the middle of nowhere, the only two people on the planet. I splash water onto her face. She closes her eyes and opens them when I stop. I tread toward the shallows, step out of the pond, and carry her into the forest.

Simone and I stand on the bank of the Kennebec River. Upstream, where water splits into three channels and flows between two gravel bars, the river is shallow enough to see bottom. In front of us the water is deeper and darker. On the opposite bank, on a slope that rises to a thin forest, a canoe is chained to a tree. Nine AM. The canoe guy isn't scheduled to arrive for another hour. Richard stumbles up and I point upstream, tell him that's the best place to ford. He was up all night, drinking and dancing around the fire. He looks at me like he hopes I'll change my mind, heads through the brush along the bank.

Simone takes off her pack and twists her back one way, then

the other. I press my palms against the tense muscles, and she lowers her head. Richard enters the river at the shallowest point, falls in the first channel, a splash that makes me laugh. He gets up and plods onward, steps onto the first gravel bar and shakes like a wet dog, water droplets reflecting the rays from the mid-morning sun.

"He's so fucking drunk he can't stand up," I say.

"I think the water's rising."

I study the river's edge, close to my feet, watch the water-line creep up a partially submerged rock. "Hey," I shout upriver. "You need to get your ass in gear."

Richard has this goofy grin, waves like he's a tourist out for a walk in the park. I drop my pack, a thud at my feet, run through the brush, and jump off the bank into the water. He starts toward me and I holler for him to get up on the second gravel bar, which is no longer above the surface but I can still see the bottom be-cause that section of river is lighter than where I stand. I power toward him, water up to my knees, walk up and over the first bar, into the middle channel. The current pushes at my legs, a force that brings with it a realization that speeds my heart. This river cares nothing about Taz Chavis, will not feel one way or the other if I drown and my body washes all the way to the Atlantic Ocean. This river flows downstream. That's what it does.

I feel small, unimportant as I step on a slippery boulder, inch sideways until my right foot finds purchase on the gravel bottom. Richard faces upstream, like he wills this onslaught to stop. I keep going until I reach the second bar and step up beside him. The water is knee-deep and rising.

"We've got to swim for it," I say.

"I don't want to go back to selling tires."

"What?"

"I hate how they smell," he says. "I hate the smell of new rubber. I hate whitewalls, radials, balancing, two-for-one sales. I hate it all."

Sand and pebbles swirl around my legs, and the water turns muddy brown.

"You're going to have to take off your pack and your boots and swim for it," I say.

He tells me he lined the inside of his pack with a garbage bag.

"My pack will float," he says.

"At least take off your boots."

"I'm not taking off my boots."

"They'll drag you to the bottom."

"If I'm going to die, I want my boots on," he says. "It's a Montana thing."

"Jump and aim for the bank."

"You jump and aim for the bank," he says.

I tell him there are worse jobs than selling tires and he asks me to name one.

"You could be in prison," I say.

"That's not a job."

"You could pump out port-o-johns for a living."

"Okay," he says. "You got me there."

Richard sucks his lips in so tight they disappear. He tells me he's staying until the water scrapes him off this sandbar and carries him downstream. By then I'll be too tired to rescue his ass so I tell him to jump, and he shakes his head. I tell him one more time, see a second shake of the head, shove him into the surging channel. He lands on his chest, a furious splash. His mouth opens, and a watery scream explodes from his lungs. I dive in and the current pushes us downstream to where the river widens and one bank is as close as the other. I holler for him to doggie paddle. Stroke in his direction. He unbuckles his pack and holds it above his head, and they both go under. He comes back up, clutches my neck, and we both go under. Bubbles swirl upward. I touch bottom and kick toward the surface and burst through. Richard's arm presses against my windpipe and spots float in front of my eyes.

I cock my fist and bring it down hard. Blood spurts out of his nose, but his eyes are still focused and he won't let go, so I hit him again. I continue to hit him, an accumulation of blows that jar him enough so his eyes roll back until only white shows and he goes limp. Which is a good thing, because I am not about to drown in this river. I curl an arm around his chest and tow him through the water. His pack drags him down, but he's clutching it so tight I can't pry the straps from his fingers and keep him afloat. A shout from the bank, and Simone ducks under a tree limb and jumps over a log. She runs through the forest, paralleling my progress, hollers at me to swim her way. One bank looks as close as the other, so I angle toward her. A rock skims across the surface.

"If you hit me with one of those, I'll beat your ass," I holler.

Another rock skips past. Richard sputters awake and I tell him to kick his feet if he wants to live, and he kicks his feet and that helps and soon we close in on the bank. I have walking muscles, not swimming muscles, and I'm slowing down.

"Who are you shouting at?" he says. "Why are you screaming in my ear?"

"Simone's throwing rocks at us."

"Oh."

That's all he says. A splash, a limb in the water, and I grab hold. Simone braces herself and hauls upward, hand over hand, until I touch bottom. I have never been so happy to have my feet under me.

Richard and I climb out of the river, and the three of us collapse on the bank. From somewhere in the forest comes the howl of a chainsaw. He turns his pack upside down and water pours out. Then he opens a bottle and pours its contents on the ground.

"I'm done drinking." Richard's chest heaves, and he swipes at snot running from his nose. "I'm giving it up for good."

Richard and I follow my girlfriend along the riverbank. I'm soaked and my trail runners squish with each step. So do Richard's boots. His nose swells, and blood falls from his nostrils to his feet. Across the river, the ferryman drags the canoe down the bank. When we reach the AT, I wave at the man and he slides the canoe in the water and paddles our way.

"I'm sorry about the rocks," Simone says.

"That's all right."

"I throw things when I get nervous."

Tears slick her cheeks.

"I thought you were going to die," she says.

12

IN CARATUNK, THE small town just north of the Kennebec River, Richard fingers his nose to the left, then to the right, winces as cartilage crackles. He watches Taz and Simone walk down the sidewalk, packs loaded with new supplies, hollers that he will catch up in a few hours. His near drowning has sobered him, and he's stayed behind because he wants to call his father or his mother or anyone back home who will pick up the phone. Simone and Taz don't turn around, and he doesn't blame them for being angry.

He sits in front of the store, a small building with local fliers on its door, drinks a Gatorade, eats a Twinkie, licks the stickiness off his fingers. There is alcohol inside the store—beer and wine—and through the window he sees the bottles on the top shelf of the cooler against the far wall. He turns and crosses his legs, his arms, exhibits the stoicism his people have shown for generations. An Indian can turn to stone if he wants. He can sit so still a bird will land on his shoulder.

A red convertible curves into the parking lot, chrome rims reflecting the sunlight, and a fat blond woman gets out and aims his way. She has on a green blouse and carries a notebook. Richard ignores her and thinks about what he will say when he makes his phone call. He doesn't think he will tell whoever is on the other end about his vow to stop drinking. Nor will he tell about his near drowning. That would make his mother and father worry, and there is no need for that kind of thing.

"Hey, are you a thru-hiker?" the blonde says.

Richard smells the stink of sweat and perfume, a white woman smell, and nods her way.

"My editor sent me over to get a story," the woman says. "I need some quotes about the trail, why you're doing it, who you are, if you've seen any bears, crap like that. . . . Hey, how'd your nose get like that?"

He wipes his nostrils with the back of his hand and stares at the blood smeared on his skin.

"I rescued someone from the Kennebec," he says. "White man named Taz Chavis, can't swim for shit."

The woman leans forward and her eyes widen. She opens her notebook, plucks a pencil from a pocket, puts the pencil away, and closes the book. "Hey, are you hungry? There's a restaurant about twenty miles up the road. Sure beats talking in this heat."

The woman—her name is Betty Ipplewell—sits across the table and writes in her notebook. It is mid-afternoon, the lunch crowd long gone, and they are the only patrons left in the place. The restaurant specializes in feeding fishermen, and antique fly rods crisscross the ceiling. Lunker rainbows on polished plaques, flies and lures dangling from rigid mouths, hang on the walls. From the kitchen comes the rattle of silverware and the murmur of conversation, kitchen help preparing for the evening rush. Richard takes a bite of spaghetti, drinks from a glass full of sweet tea. Between bites and sips, he gets out the story.

"The water came up and he was floundering like a turtle," Richard says. "He started drifting downriver and screaming and stuff. . . . I just did what anyone would do."

"Have you had lifeguard training? Anything to prepare you for the situation?"

"I'm a Blackfoot, we're the best swimmers in the world." He orders more bread sticks, chews up another bite of spaghetti. The noodles have a spicy sauce, tiny pieces of chopped up mushrooms, and the meatballs have a crunchy brown crust. This plate is his fourth and his stomach is full, yet he keeps on eating and talking. His lie gets larger, just like his stomach, and he wonders if both will get so large they explode.

Betty nibbles one of his bread sticks, and her foot brushes his. She has gray eyes, mascara on her lashes, plump cheeks that remind him of ripe peaches, but then he is always thinking about food and can't be blamed for the comparison. Her blouse is unbuttoned three times below the collar, and the tan of her bra shows against her skin. She has cleavage and Richard fantasizes licking his way to nipples large as purple grapes. He senses intense loneliness in her, the same suffocating feeling he has lived with most of his life, yet cannot bring himself to feel empathy for her plight. If she went on a diet, she could solve her problem. He, however, will be a displaced Indian until the day he dies. Their feet remain together, toe to toe, and a flush forms on her throat, red blotches that creep toward her cheeks. She is fat and smells bad, but his blood is hot and he wants to see where this will lead.

"I have a broken nose," he says.

"I see that."

"I caught an elbow when I grabbed his arm."

"You really should put ice on that," she says. "It's pretty swollen."

He likes how she worries about him and wonders if she has ever had a boyfriend.

Betty has a long-finned goldfish that swims in an aquarium in the living room, no kids. She lives in the woods, in a small house she bought off an old woman who moved to the city after her husband died. Evidence of a degree hangs in a picture frame on the wall. His host graduated from the University of Maine in 1990, a journalism major, she says. The house has striped wallpaper in the bathroom, a look Betty would like to change but claims not to have the time. He prefers not to ask questions about her personal life, thinks leaving her will be easier the less he knows, so he remains silent during the tour. In the kitchen she hands him a bag of frozen peas, suggests he hold it to his nose. The bag is cold and his nose hurts, and he does as she says until the pain goes away. He hands her the bag and she puts it back in the freezer.

"I was born on the reservation," he says. "My mother's name is Wind in Her Hair and my father's is Light Foot because he can run without making a sound."

Through the window, a channel in the flowered curtains, elongated shadows crawl across the lawn. The grass is cut close to the fence; a white woman's yard. He talks about his past, the one he made up for himself when he was a kid and realized he was different from his family, tells her about riding ponies bareback alongside cottonwood creeks and killing a cougar with a spear to enter manhood. She scribbles furiously, the pencil a blur.

He studies the fat on her sides, the way her arms bulge below the triceps, wonders how it will feel to have his red-skinned body next to hers. Soft, he thinks, like falling into a bottomless feather bed.

"So you came to the AT why?" she says.

"I walk the trail because my spirit guide suggested a journey." He does not want to tell her that he hikes because he's trying to solve an alcohol problem. She keeps asking questions, eventually winds around back to the river and his heroism.

"I cannot take the credit," Richard says.

"A true hero."

Her gaze does not leave his, a suggestion that now is the time. Richard touches her arm, a lingering that trails toward her wrist, and from her lips comes a little sigh. Her hands shake, and he thinks she does not have much experience at love. She is not the only one who smells bad—the swim in the Kennebec only washed off the worst of him—and he hints around about taking a shower together.

"I want you like you are," she says.

Richard, who thinks that is the nicest thing anyone has ever said to him, lowers his head to her chest. His earlobe, where it touches her breast, feels like a hot nickel.

That night he wakes to the remnants of a dream he has had many times. His father, clad in a purple robe, on a bejeweled throne high up in the sky, had yanked a lever that turned loose a rainstorm of tires. They had landed and bounced upward, only to fall again. There were so many of them they blocked the sun, and all the animals that inhabited the forests began to die. Richard screamed his protest, but then a Monster Truck radial hit him on the head and he fell face first and lost consciousness. Now, entwined in the sheets, naked as the day he entered the world, he gasps and slowly regains consciousness. The nightlight in the socket on the wall casts a glow over the bed, Betty's ponderous body on display, lips purring with each exhale. He is hungry, so he goes into the living room and opens his pack. Eats a candy bar he finds in his food bag. The snoring stops.

"Come back to bed," Betty says from the bedroom.

"In a minute."

In the kitchen he opens the fridge and pokes around for a soda, finds a beer on the bottom shelf. Holds the can in both hands. He had his first drink when he was nine, a swallow of Jim Beam from his father's liquor cabinet. The liquor tasted awful but he was curious and came back once a week to sample different bottles. The Wild Turkey made him want to puke, but the vodka tasted good when he mixed it with orange juice.

He developed a taste for beer when he turned twelve and found a six pack a fisherman left on the dock. Richard vomited on his tennis shoes that day, told his mother he had the flu but she smelled the beer and told his father, who said it was no big deal, that all boys experiment. His mother, who left the discipline to her husband, shook her head and retired to the rear bedroom.

Richard remembers his recent vow and desperation wells up inside him. It's a jittery feeling, a lostness that scares him enough to weaken his knees. He wants to believe Taz's theory that a person can become someone else, but experience suggests his best friend is wrong and Simone's fatalism is reality. Before he met her, he thought he drank because he hated tires. Now, after hearing her talk so convincingly about how all humans are born with a flaw that leads to their demise, he knows better. He drinks because he has an alcoholic gene. The starkness in that thought, the despair in those eight simple words, stun him and he opens the can and pours it down the sink. The act brings little solace. He has quit drinking a thousand times and is under no illusion that today is any different from yesterday.

He wants to call his father and finds the phone on an end table in the living room. His finger, red and slender, punches the wrong number and he wakes up a sleepy woman in Idaho, apologizes, and dials again.

"Who are you calling?" Betty stands at the bedroom door, sheet wrapped around her body. Her hair is tangled, evidence of last night's lovemaking.

"I'll just be a minute."

The phone rings and the familiar deep voice answers on the other end. His father, an ex-marine who has risen at 4:00 AM every day of his life since he was eighteen, is already at the office. He is the proud owner of the most popular tire store in Bozeman, loves tires so much he would rather talk about them than anything else in the world.

"Dad?" Richard says.

His father's voice comes quickly. "What is it? Is something wrong?"

Richard coughs instead of talking, and his father's voice becomes more concerned.

"Are you in jail again?" his father says. "Do you need bail money?"

"Not in jail, on the trail."

"Are you drinking?"

Richard ignores the presumption. "I'm thinking about not coming home after I summit. I'm done selling tires."

"I'm counting on you . . . so is your mother. It's your duty to take over the business. Selling tires is what our family does, son."

They talk for a while longer, his father doing most of it, then good-byes are exchanged and Richard hangs up and plops on the couch. Betty plops beside him and the sheet opens, exposes her thighs. She has black-and-blue marks above her knees, where he had gripped hard to hold on.

"You're a tire salesman," she says.

"Was. I'm something else now."

"Do you . . . umm . . . do you think you might like. . . ." She takes a breath, slowly exhales. "Do you think you might want to stay with me for a while?"

Richard thinks about her question for a long time. His thru-hike should have ended yesterday, he should have drowned in that water and if it wasn't for Taz Chavis risking his neck that's what would have happened. He misses his friends and tells the white woman he wants to leave in the morning, which by the look of the grayness outside the window isn't far off. Betty picks up her notepad and flips through it, gnaws on the eraser end of the pencil.

"Is any of this true?" she says. "Any of it at all?"

Richard crosses his legs and straightens his back. The reflection on the television shows a thin young man, upright, unmovable. Jet-black hair falls down his shoulders and gathers like horsetails on his chest. His nose is large as a walnut.

"I'm a Blackfoot," he finally says, "but you can probably cross most of the rest out."

*   *   *

On the way to Caratunk, Betty's hand creeps over and rests on his thigh. He tells her that he will visit after he summits but they both know that isn't true. She flips on the blinker, turns into the store parking lot, and he steps out. The sun is up, a red globe above the trees, and he feels the warmth on his forehead. He kisses her good-bye, puts on his pack, and hikes down the road. He walks quickly, faster than normal, knows he needs to hurry if he wants to catch up to his friends. He can feel Betty watching him, the intense energy focused on his back, but he does not turn around.

13

EXCITEMENT BOILS BENEATH the surface, something every northbounder feels in Monson, Maine. Katahdin, the summit I've walked toward for so long, seems so close I can touch it. Richard, Simone, and I stay overnight in a hostel, eat pancakes for breakfast, amble outside to a picnic table, and sort through our food for the 100-Mile Wilderness. Simone, who receives mail drops from her parents, boxes she filled before she started the trail, is so sick of eating gorp she tosses a Baggie in my direction and I add it to my pile. Richard's nose has shrunk to normal, and now cants to the right, an oddness in his otherwise symmetrical features. He has shaved his head so only a black strip remains from his brow to his neckline. The strands that fall to his back are braided into a rope thin as a buggy whip. He has not drunk a drop since he emptied the bottle on the side of the Kennebec.

"Here," Simone says, and hands Richard a Baggie filled with licorice gumdrops.

He grunts and adds them to his pile. We don't talk about the river crossing, have left it behind us like unwanted pack weight. Richard fucked up and he knows it. Simone was vindicated for suggesting we all take the canoe and she knows it. I was caught between the two and had to save his ass. There is no use bringing it up.

"My father is expecting me home the day after the summit," Richard says.

His face is a mask, eyes unblinking, jaw so tight it seems made of wood. He wraps a string of red beads around his braid, ties off the string with a square knot. He has never said what he'd rather do than sell tires, and I haven't asked. It doesn't matter, I suppose. In his mind, *anything* would be better than smelling new rubber all day long.

"He says I have to stop the 'Indian nonsense,'" Richard intones. "Says he's white and my mother is white and my brothers and sisters are white, and it's bad business for a son of his to have long hair and wear feathered headbands."

"I think you have nice hair," Simone says.

"Your old man is an asshole," I say.

Richard loads up his pack, every movement slow and determined.

"No," he says. "He's basically a nice guy who thinks it's time for me to assume my responsibilities."

The mask dissolves, and the face underneath appears in all its pliability. There is sadness in his features, hopelessness. But then the mask returns. He hoists his pack to his back.

"It's lighter without the alcohol," he says.

I shake his hand, and Simone hugs his neck. Richard wants to hike this last section alone, says he wants the solace to give him more time to think. I would prefer to summit with him, but I agreed to his wishes and Simone and I plan to stay in town for another day to give him a head start. He walks out of the yard, pauses under the shadow of a giant elm, lifts his hand and waves.

I know what he's feeling, what all thru-hikers feel at this point in their hike. The closer we get to the end, the more bittersweet the journey.

Simone and I hitch to the trail early the next day. At the first shelter, I sprawl across the planked floor, head on my pack, feet propped on the wall, and read the logbook. Richard wrote one sentence:

FUCK TIRES.

The shelter has a broom in the corner, along with a Gideon bible. Strings, threaded through tuna cans, hang from the eaves. If we planned on staying here tonight, that's where we'd hang our food bags to thwart the mice. I stretch and prop my head on my pack, move a shoulder strap that digs into my ear. Graffiti is scrawled on the ceiling.

Simone walks up, says her food weight is hurting her back, eats six brownies to lighten her load. She reads the logbook, tosses it to the rear so it won't get wet if it rains.

"I liked him better when he was drinking," she says.

The day is cloudless, and the rays coming through the branches have a yellow tint. I breathe the air, imagine golden molecules traveling through my blood stream and filling my entire body. A moth floats over the ground and lights on my shoes. The wings, thin as chartreuse tissue, slowly open and close. The movement is mesmerizing, and I watch until the moth glides into the forest. Simone and I hold hands. In my past, I never held hands. I'm still changing, I guess.

"I was thinking about after," I say. "What do you think about renting a house and moving in together?"

A squirrel jumps from branch to branch and dislodged leaves float confetti-like below the tree. My question drifts with them, suspended and unanswered.

When I was in prison and reading about hiking through the 100-Mile Wilderness, I expected one hundred miles of Maine forest, solitude, beaver ponds in the lowlands, stunning views on the mountains, a trail so beautiful it made my heart hurt. I did not expect gravel roads, chainsaws in the forest, logging trucks stirring up dust as they drive to pulp mills. Still, if it hadn't been for the gravel roads, Simone and I would never have met Charlie Evers, a southbounder who hiked in the mid-1990s.

He pulls up in a pickup and asks if we want to attend his annual trail festival, says it's a three-day party, and today is the second day, so we got lucky walking out of the woods when we did. Charlie's trail name is Ink Blot, and he has so many tattoos he's more ink than skin. He paints landscape scenes on old milk jugs and sells them in tourist shops along the coast, says he feels like he's selling out, would rather do something more avant-garde but no one buys his art. He has a mournful voice, like he lost something he'll never get back.

"My work is too dark," he says. "These days people are afraid to look inside, too afraid of what they might find."

Simone and I walk off to the side and hold a low conversation. Agree that putting off the end of our thru-hike a day or two won't matter one way or the other, so we climb into the pickup bed and travel through miles and miles of forest, to a white-sided

house set in a maple grove. Charlie parks on a driveway covered in leaves, walks us to a shaded rear yard, to where several
thru-hikers mill around tables piled high with fruit and donuts. A
drum set glitters atop a wooden stage. The hikers chatter about
what they plan for the summit. One guy—his trail name is Loose
Cannon—plans to write "The End" on his ass cheeks with a
magic marker and have someone take a picture. Sweet Dreamer,
a fine-boned woman who has a French accent, plans to kneel and
give thanks to the goddesses who helped her along her journey.

Simone and I pitch under the branches of a yellow maple. The
stakes sink easily into the soft earth. We veer toward the food,
come across a hiker on the grass, a bottle next to his head. His
long black braid, red beads intact, wraps around his throat like a
boa constrictor.

Richard.

Drunk again.

Darkness descends, and the band takes the stage. There's a fiddler, a banjo player, a lead singer—a white guy who has a grav-
elly voice like Louis Armstrong—and a drummer with sleepy
eyes and a tendency to wander from the beat. Richard weaves to
the music. He holds a bottle, is too drunk to lift it to his lips.

Simone and I go inside the house, to Charlie's studio, which
is a candle-lit room on the first floor. Our host paints faces—of
himself. Simone and I start at the doorway and walk clockwise
around the room, stop at paintings hung three feet apart.

"No wonder he can't sell his work," I say, breathing in the
smell of drying paint. "Who would buy this shit?"

Each painting has an exaggerated feature, an ear that looks

like it went through a meat grinder, an upper lip so thin and shriveled it reminds me of a dried-out green bean, a forehead so stretched out the effect is one of looking into a fun-house mirror. The portraits grow darker as we walk, the maimed body parts more exaggerated, until we come to a body-sized painting of a tattooed man that includes all that came before. Gouged eyes stare back at us, unseeing, unblinking, gore-like tears dripping down the distorted face.

Next to the door, a milk jug glows in the candlelight. A mountain landscape wraps the bottom half of the perimeter. Peaks and valleys, sun in a blue sky. Clouds suspend over the land.

Charlie walks in, head down, like he is uncomfortable watching people look at his work. Simone hugs his neck and whispers in his ear and he nods. They stay that way for at least a minute, like they are sharing a secret. Soon I'm the only motherfucker in the room who isn't crying. Charlie walks to the milk jug, crosses his tattooed arms, and stares downward. Simone stands beside him.

"It's very nice," I finally say. "Superb craftsmanship."

They look at me like that's the most ridiculous thing they have ever heard, then our host says he has to get back to his guests and abruptly walks out the door.

"What the hell was that all about?" I say.

Simone wipes her sleeve against her cheeks, and the tears dry up. "If you have to ask, you wouldn't understand."

"Try me."

"It's the first time I've ever seen anyone paint what's inside of me, Taz. It got to me, that's all."

I stare at the paintings, the grotesqueness that leers at me from all directions, turn toward the window before I say something

stupid. I don't get art, never have, and those paintings mean nothing to me. Outside, the band plays a fast tune, fiddle sweeping the
melody along. Richard has sobered up enough to start drinking,
and he sits on the stage and sips from his bottle.

"You might be right about Richard," I say.

"People stay the same. That's the irony of life."

"I'm different," I say. "I'm not the same guy that started down
in Springer."

Simone, in front of the full-sized portrait, studies me with such
intensity I cannot turn away. Her gaze has a penetrating glare,
like she can see who I was, who I am now, and who I will become.

"You only *think* you're different," she says.

Her presumption pisses me off, and I can't keep the annoyance
out of my voice. "You have no idea what you are talking about."

She walks out of the room, and through the window I watch
hikers dance around Richard like he's a goddamn icon. The fiddler whips his bow across the strings, and the drummer's sticks
slice the air. The lead singer growls his lyrics. Simone is right
about Richard. He will die a drunk, but I am not Richard. I am
Taz Chavis, and I choose dominion over my life. I am Taz Chavis, and I plan on living a good life after the trail.

Footsteps, Simone returning to apologize, but there is only an
offered plate. At first I think she has brought me a peace offering,
maybe a plate of ribs or a barbecue sandwich off the grill. I look
closer and a claw grips my heart. In the center of the plate, a line
of thin white powder beckons. I look at her face, study the smile
that contorts her lips. I hate her for this and tell her so.

"No," she says. "You only hate yourself."

I take the plate, look closer, and twist my wrist. Powder drifts
to the floor and settles around our feet.

"I don't know what that was," I say. "But—"

"It was baking soda."

"That's what I thought."

"It doesn't matter," she says. "I saw your face."

The fiddler jumps around the stage, music exploding from his strings. The hikers writhe around someone, and I think it's Richard until legs separate and I get a good look at the tattooed face. Charlie kneels, hands outstretched, beckoning the dancers until they swallow him in their midst. Simone takes my hand, leads me outside, into our tent. She is right; I don't hate her. But she is also wrong; I don't hate myself. I move on top of her, enter her with more urgency than usual, and our rhythms merge and separate. She takes my face in her hands and brings her lips close to mine.

"I want a suicide pact," she says. "You, me, and Richard."

I tremble and know she can feel it.

"Whatever it is. . . ." I say.

She pushes me off her, curls her legs to her chest, and rocks in slow motion. I lie beside her, on my sleeping bag, listen to the party outside. Richard whoops and hollers, hikers clap in rhythm. I wonder if Simone is right, if our genes set us out on an unwavering trail, that we are who we are and no amount of walking will change a thing.

Seven days after beginning the 100-Mile Wilderness, Richard, Simone, and I stealth camp in a flat spot off the trail a quarter mile up Katahdin. An evergreen thicket shields us from patrolling park rangers in the campground down below. When it becomes too dark for rising smoke to reveal our location, Richard builds a fire, using a technique, according to him, that his people perfected long before Columbus got lost and discovered America. In the crater, surrounded by mounded rocks covered with dirt, twigs crackle and burn. A dim red glow casts upward; Simone and Richard are barely visible.

They huddle across from me, and she has her arm around his neck. Their tone is urgent, words too low for me to make out.

"Hey," I say. "Does anyone want some tea?"

I boil water, make a cup, sip, and watch the smoke twist through the branches overhead.

"I think we should get some sleep," I say.

I make another cup, eat a candy bar I purchased in the store near Abol Bridge. The candy bar tastes fresh. The chocolate tastes strong. Richard gets out a bottle and firelight glints off the corners and reflects into the darkness. Nostalgia sweeps over me and I want to embrace my friends and I want them to embrace me. At that moment Georgia seems like so long ago I feel like I have walked out of one world and into another.

Another hour passes, no words aimed my way, so I pack up my stove and crawl into the tent. Simone's sleeping pad and sleeping bag are unrolled beside mine, but I do not expect her anytime soon. I am surprised when she unzips the fly a few minutes later. I ask her to talk to me, but hear nothing but silence.

In the middle of the night, I wake and go outside to piss. The air is nippy. I can see my breath, and I walk to the edge of the clearing to relieve myself. A voice comes out of the darkness. Richard, in the moonlight, sits on the trail.

"About tomorrow. . . ." Richard says.

I sit next to him.

"There's AA," I say. "Programs, rehab facilities, stuff like that."

He hands me his bottle, and I hand it back without taking a drink.

"Did you ever tell her about the dead guy we found down in Georgia?" he says.

"Are you nuts?"

"She knows about him," Richard says.

"Bullshit."

"She told me his name, when and where he died, and she knows about the others too. Remember that newspaper article about that old woman who supposedly committed suicide because her husband was dying of cancer? Simone was there, Taz. She says she pushed the woman over the edge."

"That's . . . what? You'd better be joking—"

"She knew his *fucking name*," Richard says.

I leave him on the trail and crawl into the tent. Flick a lighter, grab Simone's arm, yank it across the sleeping bag. She jerks awake, a startled look.

"What?" she says. "What do you want?"

We stare at each other, and she cannot look me in the eyes for long. When she turns her head, I flick off the lighter, and we lie in the dark. I want to ask if Richard is telling the truth, don't know exactly how to go about—

"Did you kill Christopher Orringer?" I say.

A long silence follows, and I repeat the question. Simone sobs, wracking sounds that come from her gut, and I turn away and jam my legs into my sleeping bag. Death means little to me. I've seen people shot on the streets, I've seen them stabbed in prison, I've seen a man get into an argument and run over his girlfriend, but that was the real world where bad things happen. This is the fucking Appalachian Trail, a walk through forests and rolling green pastures, across mountaintops so close to the sky at times I felt like I was a god and not a mortal strolling with a pack on my back. People die accidental deaths in the mountains, that's a risk they assume when they leave civilization, but murder is something altogether different. A hiker murdering hikers is a defilement, the worst of mankind, and what was clean and pure, my journey from Georgia, every experience along the way, is suddenly dirty, something I wish I could sweep under the rug and ignore, but there is no rug and there is no ignoring the fact that my girlfriend confessed to two murders and probably committed two more.

I grab her shoulders, shake her hard.

"What the fuck?" I say. "How could you do that to those people?"

Her sobbing continues and I clamp my hands over my ears, tell myself that I will not go back to what I was before. I repeat these words. I sharpen them until they are a tempered blade I drive into my skull. I will not go back to what I was before.

I will not.

In the early-morning hours, well before dawn, Simone crawls outside and packs up her gear. Richard does the same. Headlamp glare shines through the tent, Richard and Simone looking in my direction. Richard says good-bye, a voice barely audible, and their footsteps recede up the trail. I'd like to smash in their skulls. If Simone wants to commit suicide, that's one thing. Influencing Richard is another. There are worse things than living the life of a drunk. *Much worse* things.

I consider jogging downhill and telling a ranger what I know, but I am not a snitch. I think about packing up, chasing them down, and hauling Richard back to civilization, but I am not Gandhi. I ponder lying here for eternity, but I walked all the way from Georgia and I'll be damned if I'll allow Richard and Simone to deny my summit. I force the night's revelation from my mind, wait an hour, pack up, walk the trail. I hear their voices above me, in the darkness, occasionally glimpse a headlamp through the trees.

The air has a wet feel that thins as I walk. My pack shifts, and I reach around and pat it like an old friend. I will miss not having it back there. Trees grow small—stubby outgrowths not much higher than my waist—and soon the trail veers above tree line. Up ahead, the glow from two headlamps sweeps through the night. The half moon is low, behind a film of horizontal clouds. A car travels a road in the flatlands, headlights barely visible in low-hanging fog.

I hike upward, pausing to seek out the white blazes when I lose the trail in the rocks. A gray strip on the eastern horizon signals dawn is on its way. I wrap my hands around metal rods driven into the rock, swing myself to the left, out into open space. Although I cannot see what is beneath me, I sense a long fall. The risk, the sudden exposure jacks up my heartbeat. I hang in the air, revel in the feeling. The crawl of adrenaline through my veins feels the same as when I shot coke, and I hang for a long time before continuing up the trail.

My direction is north, to the top, but what then? I have several options, trails that take different routes off the mountain, but they all lead to civilization and a different kind of life. The stars and the moon fade, lights on the road are no longer visible. The headlamps above me switch off, and two shadowy figures toil on.

I eat a candy bar, a minty chocolate, savor the almonds in the center. My legs power upward—flesh, tendon, and bone—two pistons that will never again be as strong. A pebble works its way between my sock and my right heel, and still I hike. I enjoy the bite into my flesh. I revel in the feeling of feeling.

I whoop and hike onward. I hear nothing from above, watch Richard and Simone crest the peak and walk out of sight. I think of Roxie and hope Simone's prediction is wrong, that Roxie will stay away from coke and lead a good life. I don't know where I'm headed, but it's anywhere but Atlanta.

I reach the crest, only it's a false peak and not the summit, and I walk upward. A jet, a silver sliver on a westbound journey, rumbles across the sky. Maybe I'll fly to get where I'm going. I have enough money left from my inheritance to go first class, and I'll sit in the cabin with my worn-out shoes and backpack, a man whose smile holds more depth and knowledge than it did months ago. People will look at me and think this man next to the window knows things they don't. They will remember me long after the seat belts are fastened and dinner is served.

There is a spring beside the trail and I kneel and fill my water bottle. I drink and the wetness drips off my lips and down my cheeks. The coldness, the purity, the cleanness of taste. Sensations. That's what a thru-hike is. A string of sensations that meld into one flowing river. I laugh, think I sound like Richard.

The sun becomes a redness above the horizon, and Katahdin casts a blocky shadow to the west. The mountain towers above a fall foliage that looks brown in the early light. The only smells are my own, the accumulation of sweat on my pack, the stink of dirty socks and a dirtier body. I have grown accustomed to the unwashed during my long walk.

And then I am on top, next to the summit sign, and the rush that goes through me pounds against my temples. I look to my right, to where Richard and Simone sit on a boulder. The drop beneath their feet—a cliff that slopes 2,500 feet to Chimney Pond—is the most dramatic elevation change on the Appalachian Trail.

We are alone, the only hikers to start for the summit before daylight. Simone talks to Richard. Watches me. I jerk back to reality, a suddenness that leaves me with a churning stomach. Richard shakes his head, like he has changed his mind. He rises, this friend of mine for the last 2,160 miles.

"Don't," I say. "Don't you fucking jump, Richard."

He nods and I know it will be all right, that we'll walk off this mountain and find him a rehab, or maybe we'll walk off this mountain and keep walking. It doesn't matter. We'll walk out of here instead of choosing a solution of no return.

Simone's hand goes out and I see what is about to happen and my mouth opens and no words come out. A shove. Hard. On his left leg for he is turned away from the cliff and headed for safety. And then he is not.

Richard stumbles and steps off the edge. He looks at me, and his face transforms into a tough, unyielding veneer. I watch him tumble in a slow somersault, see his body bounce off the granite. His pack rips off his back and follows him downward. He is no doubt dead long before he splashes into Chimney Pond.

"He changed his mind!" I scream, or think I scream it because my mind has gone numb and I might not have said any such thing.

"No, he just wanted to shake your hand before he died. He admired you. Said if he was more like you he wouldn't be in the shape he was in."

"He changed his mind!"

Simone stands, edges backward until only her toes remain on this earth. Behind her, off to the right and down the mountain, small figures are beginning to show against the skyline on the Knife Edge Trail, a path that follows a thin ridge to the summit. Simone says something I can't hear, and I ask her to say it again.

"I'm not a bad person," she says. "I—"

"You murdered him!"

"None of this is my fault."

My voice is hoarse, loud, and I force my lips to form understandable words. "You *murdered* him."

The wind picks up, a steady blow from the north, and chilliness creeps in at the base of my neck. I'm having trouble sorting my thoughts. A series of trail memories, snapshots, flit through my mind. Mostly I see white blazes on trees, on rocks, on fence posts, on light poles where the trail meandered through towns. I see campsites and sunrises, taste the sweat on my lips, feel the pain that was with me during my journey. The memories have a calming effect and end with Simone and me, hip to hip, watching the sunset at Pen Mar Park. Now I focus on her, on that serious face looking my way, and say the first words that come to mind.

"We can get you help. We can walk down this mountain and work this out."

She has a curious look. "You still don't understand. I planned this from the beginning of my hike, before I ever met you. From step one on Springer, if I ended the trail as I began, I planned to jump."

"Bullshit."

"It's true."

"No," I say. "You walked this trail because you *like* pushing people over the edge."

"There is *nothing* I like about it!" Her hands turn into fists. "I *hate* this part of me."

The hikers on Knife Edge move slowly upward, tiny figures making their way one step at a time. I walk toward Simone, pass the summit sign, the symbol of the end of my journey, and I feel nothing. A bird lands on the rocks, a head that cocks to the side, beady eyes surrounded by brown feathers. I kick a rock in the bird's direction, and the bird flaps its wings and sails off the mountain and out of sight. Simone's words mix with saliva, a verbal spray in my direction.

"Don't come any closer," she says.

I continue walking, gaze on her face, my feet finding their way on their own.

"I could have killed you a hundred times," she says. "I could have waited for you in the dark this morning and shoved you over the edge."

"But you didn't."

Simone looks back and down, raises her arms to her sides.

"I was a gymnast," she says. "I had a fiancé named Devon, a better man than you, and I almost killed him."

I cover the four feet between us in one quick step, and I have one of her wrists in mine. The drop off at my feet is a startling expanse, an invitation to death. Her free hand goes to my face, a gentle touch, and she kisses me like the dead in the car wreck.

"You are doomed," Simone says.

She steps off the ledge, and the weight of her falling body slams me to my knees. I wrap an arm around a boulder, strain in the opposite direction, have no leverage, and cannot lift her even a little. She is motionless, waiting for the inevitable. I wish for a ranger to walk up, but rangers rarely stray from their vehicles and there is no help in sight. My shoulder aches, the muscles and tendons pulling downward. My arm, where it hugs the boulder, feels like one giant cramp. I scuttle my feet to the right, find a crack, and jam my toe downward. My jaw digs into the cliff, a hard granite line pushing up against the bone, and I concentrate on my grip, will it to remain strong, to hold on until a hiker walks up and gives me some help, only I know any chance of that happening is a good hour or more away. . . .

My hand slides across her fingers, and I don't know if I lost concentration or my grip weakened so much I couldn't hold on. Her fingertips leave mine and she tumbles into open space and begins a downward fall. She hits the slope, ricochets off the granite time and again, a violence that I prefer not to watch and I turn away from the edge long before she reaches bottom. The hikers on Knife Edge, tiny silhouettes against the sky, continue on, oblivious to anything but their struggle.

I walk to the summit sign and lie on the rocks, rest my head on a boulder. I have lost my best friend and my girlfriend in the space of ten minutes' time. Immense sadness comes over me, a feeling of loneliness that I doubt I'll ever shake. Simone's last words echo through my mind. I don't know if she was right or wrong about me. I might have a destructive gene or I might like coke a little too much. The end result is the same.

14

I DO NOT tell the park rangers about the dead man in Georgia, to do that would put myself in the position of explaining the funeral pyre, but I tell them everything else and I tell them in the same way again and again. The FBI performs DNA tests on fabric from the old woman in New Hampshire, and the results confirm my story.

I move into a small apartment in downtown Millinocket, an hour's drive from Katahdin, work for a small restaurant as a fry cook. I fry oysters and shrimp and fish in one fryer, french fries in the other. Pay is twelve dollars an hour, and by the time winter passes and spring begins, I receive a raise to fourteen.

On the anniversary of the start of my thru-hike, I pack my backpack and take a bus to the West, ride in silence, endure the crush of people, the stink from the restroom, the numerous town stops along the way. In Denver, I take a bus north, arrive seven hours later in Hawkinsville, Wyoming.

The depot is empty, no drunk and his dog on the sidewalk. The feed store, the mustiness, smells the same. I walk through town, pack on my back, past the bar where I stood outside and watched my father all those evenings. In the shadow of a clap-board building, a boy sits on the sidewalk and stares vacantly across the street. He wears a ripped T-shirt, has silver dumb-bells in both earlobes. I shove him with my foot and he falls to his side, gaze slowly refocusing. A crack pipe rolls in a semi-circle.

I walk down the sidewalk, past a string of buildings with glass so etched from the sand their interiors are too blurry to make out, come to a woman in a dress hiked up to her ass. She wears red stilettos and walks in small steps, asks me to buy her a drink.

"I don't drink," I say.

I walk on, feel the stretch of my legs and the swing of my arms. It feels good to be free of the bus, away from the interminable vibration of the motor, under this sunshine. I walk to the motel where the one-legged whore and I spent the night, turn onto the street where I grew up. The houses are modest one and two bed-rooms, a few have white fences around the yard. A chained pit bull growls as I walk past.

The house on the end is vacant, windows busted out, weeds high enough to cover the front steps. A bank FOR SALE sign sits in the yard. I am not surprised there have been no takers.

On the porch, I shoulder open the door. It swings freely and I step inside. Pop's pill bottles litter the floor, the sofa where he and I and my mother sat and watched television, the end tables, every available flat spot in the room. Dust covers everything. I walk to the rear of the house, down the hallway, to the closet next to his bed, stand in front of the slatted door and wonder why I am here. I have no morbid curiosity, no thrill in seeking out death, no desire to look inside and see the blood stains. The bed is made up, covers tight to the pillow, like he tried to tidy up before he died. I was conceived here, in this room connected to the closet where my father put the shotgun to his head.

I walk the road to the edge of town, step over the sand-clogged gutter and angle toward the graveyard. Pop's marker stands alone, marked by a headstone that slopes toward Hawkinsville. I step carefully through the weeds, wary of rattlesnakes, see only a lizard on a pile of rocks.

At the headstone, I kneel and shove sand under the edge, tamp it down. Try to think of something good about Pop. He was true to his job, I'll give him that. He never let a dog go, killed every last one that wasn't claimed by its owner. I wonder what he was thinking when he pulled the trigger, if he thought of me or if he thought of anything at all.

The sun is setting, a fire to the west, clouds an orange tint. Now is the time when horses come to the spring, but I don't remember how to get there. I wipe sand off my hands, watch the trickle turn to dust in the breeze. I tell Pop that I am not him, that I will never be him, that I am a different man from the boy he knew. I tell him about Richard and Simone, and how we hiked the Appalachian Trail. I tell him life never turns out like we want it. I talk to him until dark, say good-bye, and head for town. There are trails to walk. I feel them inside me, a gravity that tugs me in their direction. I need to keep moving, can't stay in one place long, and don't know why.

I do know one thing for sure. Death is not the answer.

Death is *never* the answer.

Acknowledgments

KERRI KOLEN, MY editor, brought out the best of this novel. I am humbled to have worked with her.

My heart goes out to my agent, Leigh Feldman, and I'd like to thank her for being the first person to read and believe in *Black Heart on the Appalachian Trail*. Without her I'd still be in that little attic in Virginia.

Too, I cannot forget the hard-working volunteers who maintain the Appalachian Trail. Some of these folks have maintained the AT for years, asking nothing in return. Without them the mountains would reclaim the trail and the AT would cease to exist.

I'd also like to thank the Appalachian Trail Conservancy for their ceaseless efforts. This organization does a great job creating and maintaining the wilderness experience.

About the Author

T. J. FORRESTER has been a fisherman, a subsistence farmer, a bouncer, a window washer, and a miner. He is one of the few hikers in the world to thru-hike the Appalachian Trail, the Pacific Crest Trail, and the Continental Divide Trail. He is the author of the novel *Miracles, Inc.*, and his stories have appeared in numerous literary journals.

For more information, visit www.tjforrester.com.